Proust's Princesse ... she wrote her bestseller ... ... to pass her examinations at the Sorbonne, ... write a novel. It received international acclaim ... had sold 850,000 in France alone. Her other books ... *A Certain Smile, Those Without Shadows, Aimez-vous* *Brahms...*, *La Chamade, The Heart-Keeper, Sunlight on Cold Water,* *Scars on the Soul, The Unmade Bed, The Painted Lady, The Still* *Storm, Painting in Blood, Silken Eyes* and *Incidental Music.* She was also a playwright (her plays include *Un Piano dans l'herbe* and *Zaphorie*), wrote three volumes of autobiography – the last volume, *Avec mon meilleur souvenir,* appeared in 1984. Françoise Sagan died in 2004.

AllCity Media was established in 2000 with the goal of blending memorable design and film marketing. Award-winning campaigns include the Screen International Best Poster Award winner *I am Love* and Golden Trailer Awards winner *Man on Wire,* along with other notable campaigns such as *Let Me In, The Girl with the Dragon Tattoo, Control* and *This is England.* Their website is www.allcitymedia.com

Bonjour Tristesse

FRANÇOISE SAGAN

Translated by Irene Ash

PENGUIN BOOKS

PENGUIN ESSENTIALS

Published by the Penguin Group
Penguin Books Ltd, 80 Strand, London WC2R ORL, England
Penguin Group (USA) Inc., 375 Hudson Street, New York, New York 10014, USA
Penguin Group (Canada), 90 Eglinton Avenue East, Suite 700, Toronto, Ontario, Canada M4P 2Y3
(a division of Pearson Penguin Canada Inc.)
Penguin Ireland, 25 St Stephen's Green, Dublin 2, Ireland (a division of Penguin Books Ltd)
Penguin Group (Australia), 250 Camberwell Road, Camberwell, Victoria 3124, Australia
(a division of Pearson Australia Group Pty Ltd)
Penguin Books India Pvt Ltd, 11 Community Centre, Panchsheel Park, New Delhi – 110 017, India
Penguin Group (NZ), 67 Apollo Drive, Rosedale, Auckland 0632, New Zealand
(a division of Pearson New Zealand Ltd)
Penguin Books (South Africa) (Pty) Ltd, 24 Sturdee Avenue, Rosebank, Johannesburg 2196, South Africa

Penguin Books Ltd, Registered Offices: 80 Strand, London WC2R ORL, England

www.penguin.com

First published in France by Éditions René Julliard 1954
First published in Great Britain by John Murray 1955
Published in Penguin Books 1958
This Penguin Essentials edition published 2011

1

Printed in England by Clays Ltd, St Ives plc

ISBN: 978-0-241-95156-9

www.greenpenguin.co.uk

Penguin Books is committed to a sustainable
future for our business, our readers and our
planet. This book is made from paper certified
by the Forest Stewardship Council.

Adieu tristesse
Bonjour tristesse
Tu es inscrite dans les lignes du plafond
Tu es inscrite dans les yeux que j'aime
Tu n'es pas tout a fait la misère
Car les lèvres les plus pauvres te dénoncent
Par un sourire
Bonjour tristesse
Amour des corps aimables
Puissance de l'amour
Dont l'amabilité surgit
Comme un monstre sans corps
Tête désappointée
Tristesse beau visage.

PAUL ÉLUARD
'À peine défigurée', *La vie immédiate*

PART ONE

A strange melancholy pervades me to which I hesitate to give the grave and beautiful name of sadness. In the past the idea of sadness always appealed to me, now I am almost ashamed of its complete egoism. I had known boredom, regret, and at times remorse, but never sadness. Today something envelops me like a silken web, enervating and soft, which isolates me.

That summer I was seventeen and perfectly happy. I lived with my father, and there was also Elsa, who for the time being was his mistress. I must explain this situation at once, or it might give a false impression. My father was forty, and had been a widower for fifteen years. He was young for his age, full of vitality and possibilities, and when I left school two years before, I soon noticed that he lived with a woman. It took me rather longer to realize that it was a different one every six months. But gradually his charm, my new easy life, and my own disposition led me to accept it. He was a frivolous man, clever at business, always curious, quickly bored, and attractive to women. It was easy to love him, for he was kind, generous, gay, and full of affection for me. I cannot imagine a better or a more amusing friend. At the beginning of the summer he even went so far as to ask me whether I would object to Elsa's company during the holidays. She was a tall red-haired girl, sensual and worldly, gentle, rather simple, and unpretentious; one might have come across her any day in the studios and bars of the Champs-Élysées. I encouraged

3

him to invite her. He needed women around him, and I knew that Elsa would not get in our way. In any case my father and I were so delighted at the prospect of going away together that we were in no mood to cavil at anything. He had rented a large white villa on the Mediterranean, for which we had been longing since the spring. It was remote and beautiful, and stood on a promontory dominating the sea, hidden from the road by a pine wood; a mule path led down to a tiny creek where the sea lapped against rust-coloured rocks.

The first days were dazzling. We spent hours on the beach overwhelmed by the heat and gradually assuming a healthy golden tan; except Elsa, whose skin reddened and peeled, causing her atrocious suffering. My father performed all sorts of complicated leg exercises to reduce a rounding stomach unsuitable for a Don Juan. From dawn onwards I was in the water. It was cool and transparent and I plunged wildly about in my efforts to wash away the shadows and dust of the city. I lay full length on the sand, took up a handful and let it run through my fingers in soft yellow streams. I told myself that it ran out like time. It was an idle thought, and it was pleasant to have idle thoughts, for it was summer.

On the sixth day I saw Cyril. He was sailing a small boat which capsized in front of our creek. We had a good deal of fun rescuing his possessions, during which he told me his name, that he was studying law, and was spending his holidays with his mother in a neighbouring villa. He looked typically Latin, and was very dark and sunburnt. There was something reliable and protective about him which I liked at once. Usually I avoided university students, whom I considered rough, and only interested in themselves and their own problems, which they dramatized, or used as an excuse for their boredom. I did not care for young people, I much preferred my father's friends, men of forty, who spoke to me with courtesy and tenderness, and treated me with the gentleness of a father or a lover.

But Cyril was different. He was tall and sometimes beautiful, with the sort of good looks that immediately inspire one with confidence. Although I did not share my father's aversion to ugliness, which often led us to associate with stupid people, I felt vaguely uncomfortable with anyone devoid of physical charms. Their resignation to the fact that they were unattractive seemed to me somehow indecent.

When Cyril left he offered to teach me to sail. I went up to dinner absorbed by my thoughts and hardly joined in the conversation; neither did I pay much attention to my father's nervousness. After dinner we lay in chairs on the terrace as usual. The sky was studded with stars. I gazed upwards, vaguely hoping to see a sudden, exciting flash across the heavens, but it was early in July and too soon for meteors. On the terrace the crickets were chirruping. There must have been thousands of them, drunk with heat and moonlight, pouring out their strange song all night long. I had been told they were only rubbing their wing-cases together, but I preferred to believe that it came from the throat, guttural and instinctive like the purr of a cat. We were very comfortable. Only some tiny grains of sand between my skin and my shirt kept me from dropping off to sleep. Suddenly my father coughed apologetically and sat up.

'Someone is coming to stay,' he announced.

I shut my eyes tightly. We were too peaceful, it just couldn't last!

'Hurry up and tell us who it is!' cried Elsa, always avid for gossip.

'Anne Larsen,' said my father and he turned towards me.

I could hardly believe my ears. Anne was the last person I would have thought of. She had been a friend of my mother's, and had very little connection with my father. But all the same, when I left school two years before and my father was at his wits' end about me, he had asked her to take me in hand. Within a week she had dressed me in the right clothes and taught me something of life. I remember thinking her the most wonderful person and being quite embarrassingly fond of her, but she soon found me a young man to whom I could transfer my affections. To her I owed my first glimpse of elegance and my first flirtation, and I was very grateful. At forty-two she was a most attractive woman, much sought after, with a beautiful face, proud, tired, and indifferent. This indifference was the only complaint one could make against her: she was amiable and distant. Everything about her denoted a strong will and an inner serenity which were disconcerting. Although divorced, she seemed to have no attachments; but then we did not know the same people. Her friends were clever, intelligent and discreet; ours, from whom my father demanded only good looks or amusement, were noisy and insatiable. I think she rather despised us for our love of diversion and frivolity, as she despised all extremes. We had few points of contact: she was concerned with fashion and my father with publicity, so they met occasionally at business dinners; then there was the memory of my mother, and lastly my own determined efforts to keep in touch, because although she intimidated me, I greatly admired her. In short, her sudden arrival appeared disastrous in view of Elsa's presence and Anne's ideas on education.

Elsa went up to bed after making close enquiries about Anne's social position. I remained alone with my father and moved to the steps, where I sat at his feet. He leaned forward and laid his hands on my shoulders.

'Why are you so upset, darling? You look like a little wild cat. I'd rather have a beautiful fair-haired daughter, a bit plump, with china-blue eyes and . . .'

'That's hardly the point,' I said. 'What made you invite Anne, and why did she accept?'

'Perhaps she wants to see your old father, one never knows.'

'You're not the type of man who interests Anne,' I said. 'She's too intelligent and thinks too much of herself. And what about Elsa, have you thought of her? Can you imagine a conversation between Elsa and Anne? I can't!'

'I'm afraid it hadn't occurred to me,' he confessed. 'But you're right, it's a dreadful thought! Cécile, my sweet, shall we go back to Paris?'

He laughed softly and rubbed the back of my neck. I turned to look at him. His dark eyes gleamed, funny little wrinkles marked their edges, his mouth turned up slightly. He looked like a faun. I laughed with him as I always did when he created complications for himself.

'My little accomplice,' he said. 'What would I do without you?'

From the tender inflection of his voice I knew that he would have really been unhappy. Late into the night we talked of love, of its complications. In my father's eyes they were imaginary. He refused categorically all notions of fidelity and serious commitments. He explained that they were arbitrary and sterile. From anyone else such views would have shocked me, but I knew that in his case they did not exclude either tenderness or devotion; feelings which came all the more easily to him since he was determined that they should be transient. This conception of rapid, violent and passing love affairs appealed to my imagination. I was not at the age when fidelity is attractive. I knew very little about love.

2

Anne was not due for another week, and I made the most of these last days of real freedom. We had rented the villa for two months, but I knew that once she had come it would be impossible for any of us to relax completely. Anne gave a shape to things and a meaning to words that my father and I prefer to ignore. She set a standard of good taste and fastidiousness which one could not help noticing in her sudden withdrawals, her expressions, and her pained silences. It was both stimulating and exhausting, but in the long run humiliating, because I could not help feeling that she was right.

On the day of her arrival we decided that my father and Elsa should meet her at the station in Fréjus. I absolutely refused to go with them. In desperation my father cut all the gladioli in the garden to offer her as soon as she got off the train. My only advice to him was not to allow Elsa to carry the bouquet. After they had left I went down to the beach. It was three o'clock and the heat was overpowering. I was lying on the sand half asleep when I heard Cyril's voice. I opened my eyes: the sky was white, shimmering with heat. I made no reply, because I did not want to speak to him, nor to anyone. I was nailed to the sand by all the forces of summer.

'Are you dead?' he said. 'From over there you looked as if you had been washed up by the sea.'

I smiled. He sat down near me and my heart began to beat

faster because his hand had just touched my shoulder. A dozen times during the past week my brilliant seamanship had precipitated us into the water, our arms entwined, and I had not felt the least twinge of excitement, but today the heat, my half-sleep, and an inadvertent movement had somehow broken down my defences. We looked at each other. I was getting to know him better. He was steady, and more restrained than is perhaps usual at his age. For this reason our circumstances – our unusual trio – shocked him. He was too kind or too timid to tell me, but I felt it in the oblique looks of recrimination he gave my father. He would have liked to know that I was tormented by our situation, but I was not; in fact my only torment at that moment was the way my heart was thumping. He bent over me. I thought of the past few days, of my feeling of peace and confidence when I was with him, and I regretted the approach of that wide and rather full mouth.

'Cyril,' I said. 'We were so happy . . .'

He kissed me gently. I looked at the sky, then saw nothing but lights bursting under my closed eyelids. The warmth, dizziness, and the taste of our first kisses continued for long moments. The sound of a motorhorn separated us like thieves. I left Cyril without a word and went up to the house. I was surprised by their quick return; Anne's train could hardly have arrived yet. Nevertheless I found her on the terrace just getting out of a car.

'This is like the house of the Sleeping Beauty!' she said. 'How brown you are, Cécile! I am so pleased to see you.'

'I too,' I answered, 'but have you just come from Paris?'

'I preferred to drive down, and by the way, I'm worn out.'

I showed her to her room and opened the window in the hope of seeing Cyril's boat, but it had disappeared. Anne sat down on the bed. I noticed little shadows round her eyes.

'What a delightful villa!' she said. 'Where's the master of the house?'

'He's gone to meet you at the station with Elsa.'

9

I had put her suitcase on a chair, and when I turned round I received a shock. Her face had suddenly collapsed, her mouth was trembling.

'Elsa Mackenbourg? He brought Elsa Mackenbourg here?'

I could not think of anything to reply. I looked at her, absolutely stupefied. Was that really the face I had always seen so calm and controlled? . . . She stared at me, but I saw she was contemplating my words. When at last she noticed me she turned her head away.

'I ought to have let you know sooner,' she said, 'but I was in such a hurry to get away and so tired.'

'And now . . .' I continued mechanically.

'Now what?' she said.

Her expression was interrogatory, disdainful, as though nothing had taken place.

'Well, now you've arrived!' I said stupidly, rubbing my hands together. 'You can't think how pleased I am that you're here. I'll wait for you downstairs; if you'd like anything to drink the bar is very well stocked.'

Talking incoherently I left the room and went downstairs with my thoughts in a turmoil. What was the reason for that expression, that worried voice, that sudden despondency? I sat on the sofa and closed my eyes. I tried to remember Anne's various faces: hard, reassuring; her expressions of irony, ease, authority. I found myself both moved and irritated by the discovery that she was vulnerable. Was she in love with my father? Was it possible for her to be in love? He was not at all her type. He was weak, frivolous, and sometimes unreliable. But perhaps it was only the fatigue of the journey, or moral indignation? I spent an hour in vain conjecture.

At five o'clock my father arrived with Elsa. I watched him getting out of the car. I wondered if Anne could ever love him. He walked quickly towards me, his head tilted a little backwards;

he smiled. Of course it was quite possible for Anne to love him, for anyone to love him!

'Anne wasn't there,' he called to me. 'I hope she hasn't fallen out of the train!'

'She's in her room,' I said. 'She came in her car.'

'No? Splendid! Then all you have to do is to take up the bouquet.'

'Did you buy me some flowers?' called Anne's voice. 'How sweet of you!'

She came down the stairs to meet him, cool, smiling, in a dress that did not seem to have travelled. I reflected sadly how she had appeared only when she heard the car, and that she might have done so a little sooner to talk to me; even if it had been about my examination, in which, by the way, I had failed. This last thought consoled me.

My father rushed up to her and kissed her hand.

'I spent a quarter of an hour on the station platform, holding this bunch of flowers, and feeling utterly foolish. Thank goodness you're here! Do you know Elsa Mackenbourg?'

I averted my eyes.

'We must have met,' said Anne, all amiability. 'What a lovely room I have. It was most kind of you to invite me, Raymond; I was feeling very exhausted.'

My father gave a snort of pleasure. In his eyes everything was going well. He made conversation, uncorked bottles; but I kept thinking, first of Cyril's passionate face, and then of Anne's, both with the stamp of violence on them, and I wondered if the holidays would be as uncomplicated as my father had predicted.

This first dinner was very gay. My father and Anne talked of the friends they had in common, who were few, but highly colourful. I was enjoying myself up to the moment when Anne declared that my father's business partner was an idiot. He was a man who drank a lot, but I liked him very much, and my father and I had had memorable meals in his company.

'But Anne,' I protested. 'Lombard is most amusing; he can even be very funny.'

'All the same, you must admit that he's somewhat lacking, and as for his brand of humour . . .'

'He has perhaps not a very brilliant form of intelligence, but . . .'

She interrupted me with an air of condescension:

'What you call "forms" of intelligence are only degrees.'

I was delighted with her clear-cut definition. Certain phrases fascinate me with their subtle implications, even though I may not always understand their meaning. I told Anne that I wished I could have written it down in my notebook. My father burst out laughing:

'At least you bear no resentment!'

How could I when Anne was not malevolent? I felt that she was too completely indifferent, her judgements had not the precision, the sharp edge of spite, and so were all the more effective.

The first evening Anne did not seem to notice that Elsa went quite openly into my father's bedroom. She had brought me a jersey from her collection, but would not accept any thanks; it only bored her to be thanked, she said, and as I was anyhow shy of expressing enthusiasm, I was most relieved.

'I think Elsa is very nice,' she remarked as I was about to leave the room.

She looked straight at me without a smile, seeking something in me which at all cost she wished to eradicate: I was to forget her earlier reaction.

'Oh yes, she's a charming girl . . . very *sympathique*,' I stammered.

She began to laugh, and I went up to bed, most upset. I fell asleep thinking of Cyril, probably dancing in Cannes with girls.

I realize that I have forgotten an important factor – the presence of the sea with its incessant rhythm. Neither have I remembered the four lime trees in the courtyard of a school in Provence, and their scent; and my father's smile on the station platform three years ago when I left school, his embarrassed smile because I had plaits and wore an ugly dark dress. And then in the car his sudden triumphant joy because I had his eyes, his mouth, and I was going to be for him the dearest, most marvellous of toys. I knew nothing; he was going to show me Paris, luxury, the easy life. I dare say I owed most of my pleasures of that time to money; the pleasure of driving fast, of having a new dress, buying records, books, flowers. Even now I am not ashamed of indulging in these pleasures, in fact I just take them for granted. I would rather deny myself my moods of mysticism or despair than give them up. My love of pleasure seems to be the only coherent side of my character. Perhaps it is because I have not read enough? At school one only reads edifying works. In Paris there was no time for reading: after lectures my friends hurried me off to cinemas; they were surprised to find that I did not even know the actors' names. I sat on sunny café terraces, I savoured the pleasure of drifting along with the crowds, of having a drink, of being with someone who looks into your eyes, holds your hand, and then leads you far away from those same crowds. We would walk slowly home, there under a doorway he would draw me close and embrace me: I found out how pleasant it was to be kissed. In the evenings I grew older: I went to parties with my father. They were very mixed parties, and I was rather out of place, but I enjoyed myself, and the fact that I was so young seemed to amuse everyone. When we left, my father would drop me at our flat, and then see his friend home. I never heard him come in.

I do not want to give the impression that he was vain about his affairs, but he made no effort to hide them from me, or to invent stories in order to justify the frequent presence at breakfast of a particular friend, not even if she became a member of our household (fortunately only temporarily!). In any case I would soon have discovered the nature of his relations with his 'guests', and probably he found it easier to be frank than to take the trouble to deceive me, and thereby lose my confidence. His only fault was to imbue me with a cynical attitude towards love which, considering my age and experience, should have meant happiness and not only a transitory sensation. I was fond of repeating to myself sayings like Oscar Wilde's:

Sin is the only note of vivid colour that persists in the modern world.

I made it my own with far more conviction, I think, than if I had put it into practice. I believed that I could base my life on it.

3

The next morning I was awakened by a slanting ray of hot sunshine that flooded my bed and put an end to my strange and rather confused dreams. Still half asleep I raised my hand to shield my face from the insistent heat, then gave it up. It was ten o'clock. I went down to the terrace in my pyjamas and found Anne glancing through the newspapers. I noticed that she was lightly, but perfectly, made up; apparently she never allowed herself a real holiday. As she paid no attention to me, I sat down on the steps with a cup of coffee and an orange to enjoy the delicious morning. I bit the orange and let its sweet juice run into my mouth, then took a gulp of scalding black coffee and went back to the orange again. The sun warmed my hair and smoothed away the marks of the sheet on my skin. I thought in five minutes I would go and bathe. Anne's voice made me jump:

'Cécile, aren't you eating anything?'

'I prefer just a drink in the morning.'

'To look presentable you ought to put on six pounds; your cheeks are hollow and one can count every rib. Do go in and fetch yourself some bread and butter!'

I begged her not to force me to eat, and she was just explaining how important it was when my father appeared in his sumptuous spotted dressing-gown.

'What a charming spectacle,' he said, 'two little girls sunning themselves and discussing bread and butter.'

'Unfortunately there's only one little girl,' said Anne, laughing. 'I'm your age, my dear Raymond!'

'Caustic as ever!' he said gently, and I saw Anne's eyelids flutter as if she had received an unexpected caress.

I slipped away unnoticed. On the stairs I passed Elsa. She was obviously just out of bed, with swollen eyelids, pale lips, and her skin crimson from too much sun. I almost stopped her to say that Anne was downstairs, her face trim and immaculate; that *she* would be careful to tan slowly and without damage. I nearly put her on her guard, but probably she would have taken it badly: she was twenty-nine, thirteen years younger than Anne, and that seemed to her a master trump.

I fetched my bathing suit and ran to the creek. To my surprise Cyril was already there, sitting on his boat. He came to meet me looking serious and took my hands.

'I wanted to beg your pardon for yesterday,' he said.

'It was my fault,' I replied, wondering why he was so solemn.

'I'm very annoyed with myself,' he went on, pushing the boat into the water.

'There's no reason to be,' I said lightly.

'But I am!'

I was already in the boat. He was standing in the water up to his knees, resting his hands on the gunwale as if it were the bar of a tribunal. I knew his face well enough to read his expression and realized that he would not join me until he had said what was on his mind. It made me laugh to think that at twenty-five he saw himself as a seducer.

'Don't laugh,' he said, 'I really meant it. You have no protection against me. Look at the example of your father and that woman! I might be the most awful cad for all you know.'

He was not at all ridiculous. I thought he was kind, already half in love with me, and that it would be nice to be in love with him too. I put my arm around his neck and my cheek against his. He had broad shoulders and his body felt hard against mine.

'You're very sweet, Cyril,' I murmured. 'You shall be a brother to me.'

He folded his arm round me with an angry little exclamation, and gently pulled me out of the boat. He held me close against him, my head on his shoulders. At that moment I loved him. In the morning light he was as golden, as soft, as gentle as myself. He was protecting me. As his lips touched mine we both began to tremble, and the pleasure of our kiss was untinged by shame or regret, merely a deep searching interrupted every now and then by whispers. I broke away and swam towards the boat, which was drifting out. I dipped my face into the water to refresh it. The water was green. A feeling of reckless happiness came over me.

At half past eleven Cyril left, and my father and his women appeared on the mule path. He walked between the two, supporting them, offering his hand to each in turn with a charm and naturalness all his own. Anne had kept on her beach wrap. She removed it with complete unconcern, while we all watched her, and lay down on the sand. She had a small waist and perfect legs, and, no doubt as the result of a lifetime of care and attention, her body was almost without a blemish. Involuntarily I glanced at my father, raising an eyebrow of approval. To my great surprise he did not respond, but closed his eyes. Poor Elsa, who was in a lamentable condition, was busy oiling herself. I did not think my father would stand her for another week . . . Anne turned her head towards me:

'Cécile, why do you get up so early here? In Paris you stayed in bed until midday.'

'I was working,' I said. 'It made my legs ache.'

She did not smile. She only smiled when she felt like it, never out of politeness, like other people.

'And your exam?'

'Ploughed!' I said brightly. 'Well and truly ploughed.'

'But you *must* pass it in October.'

'Why should she?' my father interrupted. 'I never got any diplomas and I live a life of luxury.'

'You had quite a fortune to start with,' Anne reminded him.

'My daughter will always find men to look after her,' said my father grandiloquently.

Elsa began to laugh, but stopped when she saw our three faces.

'She will have to work during the holidays,' said Anne, shutting her eyes to put an end to the conversation.

I gave my father a despairing look, but he merely smiled sheepishly. I saw myself in front of an open page of Bergson, its black lines dancing before my eyes, while Cyril was laughing outside. The idea horrified me. I crawled over to Anne and called her in a low voice. She opened her eyes. I bent an anxious, pleading face over her, drawing in my cheeks to make myself look like an overworked intellectual.

'Anne,' I said, 'you're not going to do that to me, make me work in this heat . . . these holidays could do me so much good.'

She stared at me for a moment, then smiled mysteriously and turned her head away.

'I shall have to make you do "that", even in this heat, as you say. You'll be angry with me for a day or two, as I know you, but you'll pass your exam.'

'There are things one cannot be made to do,' I said grimly.

Her only response was a supercilious look, and I returned to my place full of foreboding. Elsa was chattering about various festivities along the Riviera, but my father was not listening. From his place at the apex of the triangle formed by their bodies, he was gazing at Anne's upturned profile with a resolute stare that I recognized. His hand opened and closed on the sand with a gentle, regular, persistent movement. I ran down to the sea and plunged in, bemoaning the holiday we might have had. All the elements of a drama were to hand: a seducer, a demi-mondaine and a determined woman. I saw an exquisite red and blue shell on the sea-bed. I dived for it, and held it, smooth and empty, in my hand all the morning. I decided it was a lucky charm, and that I would keep it. I am surprised that I have not lost it, for I lose everything. Today it is still pink and warm as it lies in my palm, and makes me feel like crying.

4

Anne was extraordinarily kind to Elsa during the following days. In spite of the numerous silly remarks that punctuated Elsa's conversation, she never gave vent to any of those cutting phrases which were her speciality, and which would have covered the poor girl with ridicule. I was most surprised, and began to admire Anne's forbearance and generosity without realizing how subtle she was; for my father, who would soon have tired of such cruel tactics, was now filled with gratitude towards her. He used his appreciation as a pretext for drawing her, so to speak, into the family circle; by implying all the time that I was partly her responsibility, and altogether behaving towards her as if she were a second mother to me. But I noticed that his every look and gesture betrayed a secret desire for her. Whenever I caught a similar gleam in Cyril's eye, it left me undecided whether to egg him on or to run away. On that point I must have been more easily influenced than Anne, for her attitude to my father expressed such indifference and calm friendliness that I was reassured. I began to believe that I had been mistaken the first day. I did not notice that this unconcern of hers was just what provoked my father. And then there were her silences, apparently so artless and full of fine feeling, and such a contrast to Elsa's incessant chatter, that it was like light and shade. Poor Elsa! She had really no suspicions whatsoever, and although still suffering from the effects of the sun, remained her usual talkative and exuberant self.

A day came, however, when she must have intercepted a look

of my father's and drawn her own conclusions from it. Before lunch I saw her whispering into his ear. For a moment he seemed rather put out, but then he nodded and smiled. After coffee Elsa walked over to the door, turned round, and striking a languorous, film-star pose, said in an affected voice:

'Are you coming, Raymond?'

My father got up and followed her, muttering something about the benefits of the siesta. Anne had not moved, her cigarette was smouldering between her fingers. I felt I ought to say something.

'People say that a siesta is restful, but I think it is the opposite . . .'

I stopped short, conscious that my words were equivocal.

'That's enough,' said Anne dryly.

There was nothing equivocal about her tone. She had of course found my remark in bad taste, but when I looked at her I saw that her face was deliberately calm and composed. It made me feel that perhaps at that moment she was passionately jealous of Elsa. While I was wondering how I could console her, a cynical idea occurred to me. Cynicism always enchanted me by producing a delicious feeling of self-assurance and of being in league with myself. I could not keep it back:

'I imagine that with Elsa's sunburn that kind of siesta can't be very exciting for either of them.'

I would have done better to say nothing.

'I detest that kind of remark. At your age it's not only stupid, but deplorable.'

I suddenly felt angry:

'I only said it as a joke, you know. I'm sure they are really quite happy.'

She turned to me with an outraged expression, and I at once apologized. She closed her eyes and began to speak in a low, patient voice:

'Your idea of love is rather primitive. It is not a series of sensations, independent of each other . . .'

I realized how every time I had fallen in love it had been like that: a sudden emotion, roused by a face, a gesture or a kiss, which I remember only as incoherent moments of excitement. 'It is something different,' said Anne. 'There are such things as lasting affection, sweetness, a sense of loss . . . but I suppose you wouldn't understand.'

She made an evasive gesture and took up a newspaper. If only she had been angry instead of showing that resigned indifference to my emotional irresponsibility! All the same I felt she was right: that I was governed by my instincts like an animal, swayed this way and that by other people, that I was shallow and weak. I despised myself, and it was a horribly painful sensation, all the more since I was not used to self-criticism. I went up to my room in a daze. Lying in bed on my lukewarm sheet I thought of Anne's words: 'It is something different, it's a sense of loss.' Had I ever missed anyone?

The next fortnight is rather vague in my memory because I deliberately shut my eyes to any threat to our security, but the rest of the holiday stands out all the more clearly because of the rôle I chose to play in it.

To go back to those first three weeks, three happy weeks after all: when exactly did my father begin to treat Anne with a new familiarity? Was it the day he reproached her for her indifference, while pretending to laugh at it? Or the time he grimly compared her subtlety with Elsa's semi-imbecility? My peace of mind was based on the stupid idea that they had known each other for fifteen years, and that if they had been going to fall in love, they would have done so earlier. And I thought also that if it had to happen, the affair would last at the most three months, and Anne would be left with her memories and perhaps a slight feeling of humiliation. Yet all the time I knew in my heart that Anne was not a woman who could be lightly abandoned.

But Cyril was there, and I was fully occupied. In the evenings we often drove to Saint-Tropez and danced in various bars to the soft music of a clarinet. At those moments we felt we were madly in love, but by the next morning it was all forgotten. During the day we went sailing. My father sometimes came with us. He thought a lot of Cyril, especially since he had been allowed to beat him in the swimming race. He called Cyril 'my boy', Cyril called him 'sir', but I sometimes wondered which of the two was the adult.

One afternoon we went to tea with Cyril's mother, a quiet smiling old lady who spoke to us of her difficulties as a widow and mother. My father sympathized with her, looked gratefully at Anne, and paid innumerable compliments. I must say he never minded wasting his time! Anne looked on at the spectacle with an amiable smile, and afterwards said she thought her charming. I broke into imprecations against old ladies of that sort. They both seemed amused, which made me furious.

'Don't you realize how self-righteous she is?' I insisted. 'That she pats herself on the back because she feels she has done her duty by leading a respectable bourgeois life?'

'But it is true,' said Anne. 'She has done her duty as a wife and mother, as they say.'

'You don't understand at all,' I said. 'She brought up her child; most likely she was faithful to her husband, and so had no worries; she has led the life of millions of other women, and she's proud of it. She glorifies herself for a negative reason, and not for having accomplished anything.'

'Your ideas are fashionable, but you don't know what you are talking about,' Anne said.

She was probably right: I believed what I said at the time, but I must admit that I was only repeating what I had heard. Nevertheless my life and my father's upheld that theory, and Anne hurt my feelings by despising it. One can be just as attached to futilities as to anything else. I suddenly felt an urgent desire to undeceive her. I did not think the opportunity would occur so soon, nor that I would be able to seize it. Anyhow it was quite likely that in a month's time I might have entirely different opinions on any given subject. What more could have been expected of me?

5

And then one day things came to a head. In the morning
my father announced that he would like to go to Cannes
that evening to dance at the casino, and perhaps gamble as
well. I remember how pleased Elsa was. In the familiar casino
atmosphere she hoped to resume her rôle of a 'femme fatale',
slightly obscured of late by her sunburn and our semi-isolation.
Contrary to my expectation Anne did not oppose our plans;
she even seemed quite pleased. As soon as dinner was over
I went up to my room to put on an evening frock, the only
one I possessed, by the way. It had been chosen by my father,
and was made of an exotic material, probably too exotic for
a girl of my age, but my father, either from inclination or
habit, liked to give me a veneer of sophistication. I found him
downstairs, sparkling in a new dinner jacket, and I put my
arms round his neck:

'You're the best-looking man I know!'

'Except Cyril,' he answered without conviction. 'And as for
you, you're the prettiest girl I know.'

'After Elsa and Anne,' I replied, without believing it myself.

'Since they're not down yet, and have the cheek to keep us
waiting, come and dance with your rheumaticky old father!'

Once again I felt the thrill that always preceded our evenings
out together. He really had nothing of an old father about him.
While dancing I inhaled the warmth of his familiar perfume, eau

de cologne and tobacco. He danced slowly with half-closed eyes, a happy, irrepressible little smile, like my own, on his lips.

'You must teach me the bebop,' he said, forgetting his talk of rheumatism.

He stopped dancing to welcome Elsa with polite flattery. She came slowly down the stairs in her green dress, a conventional smile on her face, her casino smile. She had made the most of her lifeless hair and scorched skin, but the result was more meretricious than brilliant. Fortunately she seemed unaware of it.

'Are we going?'

'Anne's not here yet,' I remarked.

'Go up and see if she's ready,' said my father. 'It will be midnight before we get to Cannes.'

I ran up the stairs, getting somewhat entangled with my skirt, and knocked at Anne's door. She called to me to come in, but I stopped on the threshold. She was wearing a grey dress, a peculiar grey, almost white, which, when it caught the light, resembled the colour of the sea at dawn. She seemed to me the personification of mature charm.

'Oh Anne, what a magnificent dress!' I said.

She smiled into the mirror as one smiles at a person one is about to leave.

'This grey is a success,' she said.

'You are a success!' I answered.

She pinched my ear, her eyes were dark blue, and I saw them light up with a smile.

'You're a dear child, even though you can be tiresome at times.'

She went out in front of me without a glance at my dress. In a way I was relieved, but all the same it was mortifying. I followed her down the stairs and I saw my father coming to meet her. He stopped at the bottom, his foot on the first step, his face raised. Elsa was looking on. I remember the scene perfectly. First of all, in front of me, Anne's golden neck and perfect shoulders, a little lower down my father's fascinated face and extended hand, and, already in the distance, Elsa's silhouette.

'Anne, you are wonderful!' said my father.

She smiled as she passed him and took her coat.

'Shall we meet there?' she asked. 'Cecile, will you come with me?'

She let me drive. At night the road appeared so beautiful that I went slowly. Anne was silent; she did not even seem to notice the blaring wireless. When my father's car passed us at the bend she remained unmoved. I felt I was out of the race, watching a performance in which I could no longer intervene.

At the casino my father saw to it that we soon lost sight of each other. I found myself at the bar with Elsa and one of her acquaintances, a half-tipsy South American. He was connected with the stage and had such a passionate love for it that even in his inebriated condition he could remain amusing. I spent an agreeable hour with him, but Elsa was bored. She knew one or two big names, but that was not her world. All of a sudden she asked me where my father was, as if I had some means of knowing. She then left us. The South American seemed put out for a moment, but another whisky set him up again. My mind was a blank. I was quite light-headed, for I had been drinking with him out of politeness. It became grotesque when he wanted to dance. I was forced to hold him up and to extricate my feet from under his, which required a lot of energy. We laughed so much that when Elsa tapped me on the shoulder and I saw her Cassandra-like expression, I almost felt like telling her to go to the devil.

'I can't find them,' she said.

She looked utterly distraught. Her powder had worn off leaving her skin shiny, her features were drawn; she was a pitiable sight. I suddenly felt very angry with my father; he was being most unkind.

'Ah, I know where they are,' I said, smiling as if I referred to something quite ordinary about which she need have no anxiety. 'I'll soon be back.'

Deprived of my support, the South American fell into Elsa's arms and seemed comfortable enough there. I reflected somewhat sadly that she was more experienced than I, and that I could not very well bear her a grudge.

The casino was big, and I went all round it twice without any success. I scanned the terrace and at last thought of the car. It took me some time to find it in the car park. They were inside. I approached from behind and saw them through the rear window. Their profiles were very close together and very serious, and looked strangely beautiful in the lamplight. They were facing each other and must have been talking in low tones, for I saw their lips move. I would have liked to go away again, but the thought of Elsa made me open the door. My father had his hand on Anne's arm, and they scarcely noticed me.

'Are you having a good time?' I asked politely.

'What is the matter?' said my father irritably. 'What are you doing here?'

'And you? Elsa has been searching for you everywhere for the past hour.'

Anne turned her head slowly and reluctantly towards me.

'We're going home. Tell her I was tired and your father drove me back. When you've had enough take my car.'

I was trembling with indignation and could hardly speak:

'Had enough? But you don't realize what you're saying, it's disgusting!'

'What is disgusting?' asked my father with astonishment.

'You take a red-haired girl to the seaside, expose her to the hot sun which she can't stand, and when her skin has all peeled you abandon her. It's altogether too simple! What on earth shall I say to Elsa?'

Anne turned to him with an air of weariness. He smiled at her, obviously not listening. My exasperation knew no bounds:

'I shall tell Elsa that my father has found someone else to sleep with, and that she had better come back some other time. Is that right?'

My father's exclamation and Anne's slap were simultaneous. I hurriedly withdrew my head from the car-door. She had hurt me.

'Apologize at once!' said my father.

I stood motionless, with my thoughts in a whirl. Noble attitudes always occur to me too late.

'Come here,' said Anne.

She did not sound menacing, and I went closer. She put her hand against my cheek and spoke slowly and gently as if I were rather simple:

'Don't be naughty. I'm very sorry for Elsa, but you are tactful enough to arrange everything for the best. Tomorrow we'll discuss it. Did I hurt you very much?'

'Not at all,' I said politely. Her sudden gentleness after my intemperate rage made me want to burst into tears. I watched them drive away, feeling completely deflated. My only consolation was the thought of my tactfulness.

I walked slowly back to the casino, where I found Elsa with the South American clinging to her arm.

'Anne wasn't well,' I said in an off-hand manner. 'Papa had to take her home. What about a drink?'

She looked at me without answering, I tried to find a more convincing explanation:

'She was awfully sick,' I said. 'It was ghastly, her dress is ruined.' This detail seemed to me to make my story more plausible, but Elsa began to weep quietly and sadly. I did not know what to do.

'Oh, Cécile, we were so happy!' she said, and her sobs redoubled in intensity. The South American began to cry, repeating, 'We were so happy, so happy!' At that moment I heartily detested Anne and my father. I would have done anything to stop Elsa from crying, her eyeblack from running, and the South American from howling.

'Nothing is settled yet, Elsa. Come home with me now!'

'No! I'll fetch my suitcases later,' she sobbed. 'Goodbye, Cécile, we got on well together, didn't we?'

We had never talked of anything but clothes or the weather, but still it seemed to me that I was losing an old friend. I quickly turned away and ran to the car.

6

The following morning was wretched, probably because of the whisky I had drunk the night before. I awoke to find myself lying across my bed in the dark; my tongue heavy, my limbs unbearably damp and sticky. A single ray of sunshine filtered through the slats of the shutters and I could see a million motes dancing in it. I felt no desire to get up, nor to stay in bed. I wondered how Anne and my father would look if Elsa were to turn up that morning. I forced myself to think of them in order to be able to get out of bed without effort. At last I managed to stand up on the cool stone floor. I was giddy and aching. The mirror reflected a sad sight; I leant against it and peered at those dilated eyes and dry lips, an unknown face; mine? If I was weak and cowardly, could it be because of those lips, the particular shape of my body, these odious, arbitrary limits? And if I were limited, why had I only now become aware of it? I amused myself by detesting my reflection, hating that wolf-like face, hollow and worn by debauch. I repeated the word 'debauch' dumbly, looking into my eyes in the mirror, and suddenly I saw myself smile. What a debauch! A few unfortunate drinks, a slap in the face and some tears! I brushed my teeth and went downstairs.

My father and Anne were already on the terrace sitting beside each other in front of their breakfast tray. I sat down opposite them, muttering a vague 'good morning'. A feeling of shyness made me keep my eyes lowered, but after a time, as they remained

silent I was forced to look at them. Anne appeared tired, the only
sign of a night of love. They were both smiling happily, and I
was very much impressed, for happiness has always seemed to
me a great achievement.

'Did you sleep well?' asked my father.

'Not too badly,' I replied. 'I drank a lot of whisky last night.'

I poured out a cup of coffee, but after the first sip I quickly
put it down. Their silence had a waiting quality that made me
feel uneasy. I was too tired to bear it for long.

'What's the matter? You look so mysterious.'

My father lit a cigarette, making an obvious effort to seem
unconcerned, and for once in her life Anne seemed embarrassed.

'I would like to ask you something,' she said at last.

'I suppose you want me to take another message to Elsa?' I
said, imagining the worst.

She turned towards my father:

'Your father and I want to get married,' she said.

I stared first at her, then at my father. I half expected some
sign from him, perhaps a wink, which, though I might have found
it shocking, would have reassured me, but he was looking down
at his hands. I said to myself 'it can't be possible!', but I already
knew it was true.

'What a good idea!' I said to gain time.

I could not understand how my father, who had always set
himself so obstinately against marriage and its chains, could
have decided on it in a single night. We were about to lose our
independence. I could visualize our future family life, a life which
would suddenly be given equilibrium by Anne's intelligence and
refinement; the life I had envied her. We would have clever tactful
friends, and quiet pleasant evenings . . . I found myself despising
noisy dinners, South Americans and girls like Elsa. I felt proud
and superior.

'It's a very, very good idea,' I repeated, and I smiled at them.

'I knew you'd be pleased, my pet,' said my father.

He was relaxed and delighted. Anne's face, subtly changed by love, seemed gentler, making her appear more accessible than she had ever been before.

'Come here, my pet,' said my father; and holding out his hands, he drew me close to them both. I was half-kneeling in front of them, while they stroked my hair and looked at me with tender emotion. But I could not stop thinking that although my life was perhaps at that very moment changing its whole course, I was in reality nothing more than a kitten to them, an affectionate little animal. I felt them above me, united by a past and a future, by ties that I did not know and which could not hold me. But I deliberately closed my eyes and went on playing my part, laying my head on their knees and laughing. For was I not happy? Anne was all right, I had no serious fault to find with her. She would guide me, relieve me of responsibility, and be at hand whenever I might need her. She would make both my father and me into paragons of virtue.

My father got up to fetch a bottle of champagne. I felt sickened. He was happy, which was the chief thing, but I had so often seen him happy on account of a woman.

'I was rather frightened of you,' said Anne.

'Why?' I asked. Her words had given me the impression that a veto from me could have prevented their marriage.

'I was afraid of your being frightened of me,' she said laughing.

I began to laugh too, because actually I was a little scared of her. She wanted me to understand that she knew it, and that it was unnecessary.

'Does the marriage of two people like ourselves seem ridiculous to you?'

'You're not old,' I said emphatically, as my father came dancing back with a bottle in his hand.

He sat down next to Anne and put his arm round her shoulders. She moved nearer to him and I looked away in embarrassment. She was no doubt marrying him for just that; for his laughter, for the firm reassurance of his arm, for his vitality, his warmth. At forty there could be the fear of solitude, or perhaps a last upsurge of the senses . . . I had never thought of Anne as a woman, but as an entity. I had seen her as a self-assured, elegant, and clever person, but never weak or sensual. I quite understood that my father felt proud, the self-satisfied, indifferent Anne Larsen was going to marry him. Did he love her, and if so, was he capable of loving her for long? Was there any difference between this new feeling and the affection he had shown Elsa? The sun was making my head spin, and I shut my eyes. We were all three on the terrace, full of reserves, of secret fears, and of happiness.

Elsa did not come back just then. A week flew by, seven happy, agreeable days, the only ones. We made elaborate plans for furnishing our home, and discussed timetables which my father and I took pleasure in cutting as fine as possible with the blind obstinacy of those who have never had any use for them. Did we ever believe in them for one moment? Did my father really think it possible to have lunch every day at the same place at 12.30 sharp, to have dinner at home, and not to go out afterwards? However, he gaily prepared to inter Bohemianism, and began to preach order, and to extol the joys of an elegant, organized bourgeois existence. No doubt for him, as well as for myself, all these plans were merely castles in the air.

How well I remember that week! Anne was relaxed, confident, and very sweet; my father loved her. I saw them coming down in the mornings, leaning on each other, laughing gaily, with shadows under their eyes, and I swear that I should have liked nothing better than that their happiness should last all their lives. In the evening we often drank our apéritif sitting on some café terrace by the sea. Everywhere we went we were taken for a happy, normal family, and I, who was used to going out alone with my father and seeing the knowing smiles, and malicious or pitying glances, was delighted to play a rôle more suitable to my age. They were to be married on our return to Paris.

Poor Cyril had witnessed the transformation in our midst with a certain amazement, but he was comforted by the thought that this time it would be legalized. We went out sailing together and kissed when we felt inclined, but sometimes during our embraces I thought of Anne's face as I saw it in the mornings, with its softened contours. I recalled the happy nonchalance, the languid grace that love imparted to her movements, and I envied her. One can grow tired of kissing, and no doubt if Cyril had not been so fond of me I would have become his mistress that week.

At six o'clock, on our return from the islands, Cyril would pull the boat into the sand. We would go up to the house through the pine wood in single file, pretending we were Indians, or run handicap races to warm ourselves up. He always caught me before we reached the house and would spring on me with a shout of victory, rolling me on the pine needles, pinning my arms down and kissing me. I can still remember those light, breathless kisses, and Cyril's heart beating against mine in rhythm with the soft thud of the waves on the sand. Four heart-beats and four waves, and then gradually he would regain his breath and his kisses would become more urgent, the sound of the sea would grow dim and give way to the pulse in my ears.

One evening we were surprised by Anne's voice. Cyril was lying close to me in the red glow of the sunset. I can understand that Anne might have been misled by the sight of us there in our scanty bathing things. She called me sharply.

Cyril bounded to his feet, naturally somewhat ashamed. Keeping my eyes on Anne, I slowly got up in my turn. She faced Cyril, and looking right through him spoke in a quiet voice: 'I don't wish to see you again.'

He made no reply, but bent over and kissed my shoulder before departing. I felt surprised and touched, as if his gesture had been a sort of pledge. Anne was staring at me with the same grave and detached look, as though she were thinking of something else. Her manner infuriated me. If she was so deep in thought, why speak at all? I went up to her, feigning embarrassment for the sake of politeness. At last she seemed to notice me and mechanically removed a pine needle from my neck. I saw her face assume its beautiful mask of disdain, that expression of weariness and disapproval which became her so well, and which always frightened me a little.

'You should know that such diversions usually end up in a nursing home.'

She stood there looking straight at me as she spoke, and I was horribly ashamed. She was one of those women who can stand perfectly still while they talk; I always needed the support of a chair, or some object to hold like a cigarette, or the distraction of swinging one leg over the other and watching it move.

'You mustn't exaggerate,' I said with a smile. 'I was only kissing Cyril, and that won't lead me to any nursing home.'

'Please don't see him again,' she said, as if she did not believe me. 'Do not protest: you are seventeen and I feel a certain responsibility for you now. I'm not going to let you ruin your life. In any case you have work to do, and that will occupy your afternoons.'

She turned her back on me and walked towards the house in her nonchalant way. A paralysing sense of calamity kept me rooted to the spot. She had meant every word; what was the use of arguments or denials when she would receive them with the sort of indifference that was worse than contempt, as if I did not even exist, as if I were something to be squashed underfoot, and not myself, Cécile, whom she had always known. My only hope now was my father; surely he would say as usual: 'Well now, who's

the boy? I suppose he's a handsome fellow, but beware, my girl!'
If he did not react like this, my holidays would be ruined.

Dinner was a nightmare. Not for one moment had Anne
suggested that she would not tell my father anything if I prom-
ised to work; it was not in her nature to bargain. I was pleased
in one way, but also disappointed that she had deprived me of
a chance to despise her. As usual she avoided a false move, and
it was only when we had finished our soup that she seemed to
remember the incident.

'I do wish you'd give your daughter some advice, Raymond. I
found her in the wood with Cyril this evening, and they seemed
to be going rather far.'

My father, poor man, tried to pass the whole thing off as a
joke.

'What's that you say? What were they up to?'

'I was kissing him,' I said. 'And Anne thought . . .'

'I never thought anything at all,' she interrupted. 'But it might
be a good idea for her to stop seeing him for a time and to work
at her philosophy instead.'

'Poor little thing!' said my father. 'After all Cyril's a nice boy,
isn't he?'

'And Cécile is a nice girl,' said Anne. 'That's why I should be
heartbroken if anything should happen to her, and it seems to
me inevitable that it will, if you consider what complete freedom
she enjoys here, and that they are constantly together and have
nothing whatever to do. Don't you agree?'

At her last words I looked up and saw that my father was
very perturbed.

'You are probably right,' he said. 'After all, you ought to do
some work, Cécile. You surely don't want to fail in philosophy
and have to take it again?'

'What do you think I care?' I answered.

He glanced at me and then turned away. I was bewildered. I

realized that procrastination can rule our lives, yet not provide us with any arguments in its defence.

'Listen,' said Anne, taking my hand across the table. 'Won't you exchange your rôle of a wood nymph for that of a good schoolgirl for one month? Would it be so serious?'

They both looked at me expectantly; seen in that light, the argument was simple enough. I gently withdrew my hand.

'Yes, very serious,' I said, so softly that they did not hear it, or did not want to.

The following morning I came across a phrase from Bergson:

Whatever irrelevance one may at first find between the cause and the effects, and although a rule of guidance towards an assertion concerning the root of things may be far distant, it is always in a contact with the generative force of life that one is able to extract the power to love humanity.

I repeated the phrase, quietly at first, so as not to get agitated, then in a louder voice. I held my head in my hands and looked at the book with great attention. At last I understood it, but I felt as cold and impotent as when I had read it the first time. I could not continue. With the best will in the world I applied myself to the next lines, and suddenly something arose in me like a storm and threw me on to the bed. I thought of Cyril waiting for me down in the creek, of the swaying boat, of the pleasure of our kisses, and then I thought of Anne, but in a way that made me sit up on my bed with a fast-beating heart, telling myself that I was stupid, monstrous, nothing but a lazy, spoilt child, and had no right to have such thoughts. But all the same, in spite of myself I continued to reflect that she was dangerous, and that I must get rid of her. I thought of the lunch I had endured with clenched teeth, tortured by a feeling of resentment for which I despised and ridiculed myself. Yes, it was for this I reproached Anne: she prevented me from liking myself. I, who was so naturally meant for happiness and gaiety, had been forced by her into a world of self-criticism and guilty conscience, where, unaccustomed to introspection, I was completely lost. And what did she bring me? I took stock: She wanted my father; she had got him. She would gradually make of us the husband and step-daughter of Anne Larsen; that is to say, she would turn us into two civilized, well-behaved and happy people. For she would certainly make us happy. How easily, unstable and irresponsible as we were, we would yield to her influence, and be drawn into the attractive framework of her orderly plan of living. She was much too efficient: already my father was estranged from me. I was obsessed by his embarrassed face turning away from me at table. Tears came into my eyes at the thought of the jokes we used to have together, our laughter as we drove home at dawn through the empty streets of Paris. All that was over. In my turn I would be influenced, re-orientated, remodelled by Anne. I would not even mind it, she would act with intelligence, irony and sweetness, and I would be incapable of resistance; in six months I should no longer even wish to resist.

At all costs I must take steps to regain my father and our former life. How infinitely desirable those two years suddenly appeared to me, those happy years I was so willing to renounce the other day . . . the liberty to think, even to think wrongly or not at all, the freedom to choose my own life, to choose myself. I cannot say 'to be myself', for I was only soft clay, but still I could refuse to be moulded.

I realize that one might find complicated motives for this change in me, one might endow me with spectacular complexes: such as an incestuous love for my father, or a morbid passion for Anne, but I know the true reasons were the heat, Bergson, and Cyril, or at least his absence. I dwelt on this all the afternoon in a most unpleasant mood, induced by the discovery that we

were entirely at Anne's mercy. I was not used to reflection, and
it made me irritable. At dinner, as in the morning, I did not open
my mouth. My father thought it appropriate to chaff me:

'What I like about youth is its spontaneity, its gay conversation.'

I was trembling with rage. It was true that he loved youth; and
with whom could I have talked if not with him? We had discussed
everything together: love, death, music. Now he himself had
disarmed and abandoned me. Looking at him I thought: 'You
don't love me any more, you have betrayed me!' I tried to make
him understand without words how desperate I was. He seemed
suddenly alarmed; perhaps he understood that the time for joking
was past, and that our relationship was in danger. I saw him
stiffen, and it appeared as though he were about to ask a question. Anne turned to me:

'You don't look well. I feel sorry now for making you
work.'

I did not reply. I felt too disgusted that I had got myself
into a state which I could no longer control. We had finished
dinner. On the terrace, in the rectangle of light projected from
the dining-room window, I saw Anne's long nervous hand reach
out to find my father's. I thought of Cyril. I would have liked
him to take me in his arms on that moonlight terrace, alive with
crickets. I would have liked to be caressed, consoled, reconciled
with myself. My father and Anne were silent, they had a night
of love to look forward to; I had Bergson. I tried to cry, to feel
sorry for myself, but in vain; it was already Anne for whom I
was sorry, as if I were certain of victory.

PART TWO

I

I am surprised how clearly I remember everything from that moment. I acquired an added awareness of other people and of myself. Until then I had always been spontaneous and light-hearted, but the last few days had upset me to the extent of forcing me to reflect and to look at myself with a critical eye. However, I seemed to come no nearer to a solution of my problems. I kept telling myself that my feelings about Anne were mean and stupid, and that my desire to separate her from my father was vicious. Then I would argue that after all I had every right to feel as I did. For the first time in my life I was divided against myself. Up in my room I reasoned with myself for hours on end in an attempt to discover whether the fear and hostility which Anne inspired in me were justified, or if I were merely a silly, spoilt, selfish girl in a mood of sham independence.

In the meantime I grew thinner every day. On the beach I did nothing but sleep, and at meal-times I maintained a strained silence that ended by making the others feel uneasy. And all the time I watched Anne. At dinner I would say to myself, 'Doesn't every movement she makes prove how much she loves him? Could anyone be more in love? How can I be angry with her when she smiles at me with that trace of anxiety in her eyes?' But suddenly she would say, 'When we get home, Raymond . . .' and the thought that she was going to share our life and interfere with us would arouse me again. Once more she seemed calculating and cold. I thought: 'She is cold, we are warm-hearted, she is possessive, we are independent. She is indifferent; other people don't interest her, we love them. She is reserved, we are gay. We are full of life and she will slink in between us with her sobriety; she will warm herself at our fire and gradually rob us of our enthusiasm; like a beautiful serpent she will rob us of everything.' I repeated 'a beautiful serpent' . . . she passed me the bread, and suddenly I came to my senses. 'But it's crazy,' I thought. 'That's Anne, your friend who was so kind to you, who is so clever. Her aloofness is a mere outward form, there's nothing calculated about it, her indifference shields her from the countless sordid things in life, it's a sign of nobility.' A beautiful serpent . . . I felt myself turn pale with shame. I looked at her, silently imploring her forgiveness. At times she noticed my expression and a shadow of surprise and uncertainty clouded her face and made her break off in the middle of a sentence. Her eyes turned instinctively to my father; but his glance held nothing but admiration or desire, he did not understand the cause of her disquiet. Little by little I made the atmosphere unbearable, and I detested myself for it.

My father suffered as much as his nature permitted, that is to say hardly at all, for he was mad about Anne, madly proud and happy, and nothing else existed for him. However, one day when I was dozing on the beach after my morning bathe, he sat down next to me and looked at me closely. I felt his eyes upon me, and with the air of false gaiety that was fast becoming a habit I was just going to ask him to come in for a swim when he put his hand on my head and called to Anne in a doleful voice:

'Come over here and have a look at this creature; she's as thin as a rake. If this is the effect work has on her, she'll have to give it up!'

He thought that would settle everything, and no doubt it would have done so ten days earlier. But now I was too deeply immersed in complications, and the hours set aside for work in the afternoons no longer bothered me, especially as I had not opened a book since Bergson.

Anne came up to us. I remained lying face down on the sand listening to the muffled sound of her footsteps. She sat on my other side.

'It certainly doesn't seem to agree with her,' she said. 'But if she really did work instead of walking up and down in her room . . .'

I had turned round and was looking at them. How did she know that I was not working? Perhaps she had even read my thoughts? I believed her to be capable of anything.

I protested:

'I don't walk up and down in my room!'

'Do you miss that boy?' asked my father.

'No!'

This was not quite true, but I certainly had had no time to think of Cyril.

'But still, you're not well,' said my father firmly. 'Anne, do you notice it too? She looks like a chicken that has been drawn and then put to roast in the sun.'

'Make an effort, Cécile dear,' said Anne. 'Do a little work and try to eat a lot. That exam is important . . .'

'I don't care a hang about the exam!' I cried. 'Can't you understand? I just don't care!'

I looked straight at her, despairingly, so that she should realize that something more serious than my examination was at stake. I longed for her to ask me: 'Well, what is it?' and ply me with questions, and force me to tell her everything: then I would be won over and she could do anything she liked with me, and I should no longer be in torment. She looked at me attentively. I could see the Prussian blue of her eyes darken with concentration and reproach. Then I understood that it would never occur to her to question me and so deliver me from myself, because even if the thought had entered her head, her code of behaviour would have precluded it. And I saw too that she had no idea of the tumult within me, or even if she had, her attitude would have been one of indifference and disdain, which was in any case what I deserved! Anne always gave everything its exact value, that is why I could never come to an understanding with her.

I dropped back on to the sand and laid my cheek against its soft warmth. I sighed deeply and began to tremble. I could feel Anne's hand, tranquil and steady, on the back of my neck, holding me still for a moment, just long enough to stop my nervous tremor.

'Don't complicate life for yourself,' she said. 'You've always been so contented and lively, and had no head for anything serious. It doesn't suit you to be pensive and sad.'

'I know that,' I answered. 'I'm just a thoughtless healthy young thing, brimful of gaiety and stupidity!'

'Come and have lunch,' she said.

My father had moved away from us; he detested that sort of discussion. On the way back he took my hand and held it. His hand was firm and comforting: it had dried my tears after my first disappointment in love, it had closed over mine in moments of tranquillity and perfect happiness, it had stealthily pressed mine at times of complicity or riotous laughter. I thought of his hand on the steering wheel, or holding the keys at night and searching in vain for the lock; his hand on a woman's shoulder, or holding a cigarette, the hand that could do nothing more for me. I gave it a hard squeeze. Turning towards me, he smiled.

2

Two days went by: I went round in circles, I wore myself out, but I could not free myself from the haunting thought that Anne was about to wreck our lives. I did not try to see Cyril; he would have comforted me and made me happier, but that was not what I wanted. I even got a certain satisfaction from asking myself insoluble questions, by reminding myself of days gone by, and dreading those to come. It was very hot; my room was in semi-darkness with the shutters closed, but even so the air was unbearably heavy and damp. I lay on my bed staring at the ceiling, hardly moving except to search for a cool place on the sheet. I did not sleep, but played records on the gramophone at the foot of my bed. I chose slow rhythms, without any tune. I smoked a good deal and felt decadent, which gave me pleasure. But I was not deluded by this game of pretence: I was sad and bewildered.

One afternoon the maid knocked at my door and announced with an air of mystery: 'Someone's downstairs.' I at once thought of Cyril and went down. It was not Cyril, but Elsa. She greeted me effusively. Looking at her, I was astonished at her new beauty. She was tanned at last, evenly and smoothly, and was carefully made up and brilliantly youthful.

'I've come to fetch my suitcase,' she explained. 'Juan bought me a few dresses, but not enough, and I need my things.'

I wondered for a moment who Juan could be, but did not enquire further. I was pleased Elsa had come back. She brought

47

with her the aura of a kept woman, of bars, of gay evenings, which reminded me of happier days. I told her how glad I was to see her again, and she assured me that we had always got on so well together because we had common interests. I suppressed a slight shudder and suggested that we should go up to my room to avoid meeting Anne and my father. When I mentioned my father she made an involuntary movement with her head, and I wondered whether perhaps she was still in love with him, in spite of Juan and the dresses. I also thought that three weeks before I would not have noticed that movement of hers.

In my room I listened while she described in glowing terms her smart and dizzy life in the fashionable places along the Riviera. A strange confusion of thoughts went through my head, partly suggested by her different appearance. At last she stopped talking, perhaps because I was silent. She took a few steps across the room, and without turning round asked in an off-hand way if Raymond was happy. In a moment I knew what I must say to her:

'"Happy" is saying too much! Anne doesn't give him a chance to think otherwise. She is very clever.'

'Very!' sighed Elsa.

'You'll never guess what she's persuaded him to do ... she's going to marry him ...'

Elsa turned a horrified face towards me:

'Marry him? Raymond actually wants to get married?'

'Yes,' I answered. 'Raymond is going to be married.'

A sudden desire to laugh caught me by the throat. My hands were shaking. Elsa seemed prostrated, almost as if I had given her a knockout blow. On no account must she be allowed to realize that after all he was of an age to marry, and could not be expected to spend his life with women of her sort. I leant forward and suddenly lowered my voice to make a stronger impression on her:

'It simply mustn't happen, Elsa. He's suffering already. It's an impossible state of affairs, as you can very well imagine.'

'Yes,' she said.

She seemed fascinated.

'You're just the person I've been waiting for,' I went on, 'because you are the only one who is a match for Anne. You alone are up to her standard.'

She seemed to swallow the bait.

'But if he's marrying her it must be because he loves her?' she objected.

'But look here, Elsa, it's you he loves! Do you want to make me believe that you don't know it?'

I saw her bat her eyelids, and she turned away to hide her pleasure, and the hope my words had given her. I was prompted by a sort of infallible instinct and I knew just how to continue.

'Don't you see? Anne kept harping on the bliss of married life, morality, and all that, and in the end she caught him.'

I was surprised at my own words. For even though I had expressed myself somewhat crudely, that was just what I felt.

'If they get married, our lives will be ruined, Elsa! My father must be protected, he's nothing but a big baby . . .'

I repeated 'a big baby' with stronger emphasis. It seemed to me that I was being rather too melodramatic, but I saw Elsa's beautiful green eyes fill with pity, and I ended up, like in a canticle:

'Help me, Elsa! It's for your own sake, for my father, and for the love between you.'

I added to myself: 'and for Johnny Chinaman!'

'But what can I do?' asked Elsa. 'It seems an impossible situation.'

'If you think it's impossible, then give up the idea,' I said sadly.

'What a bitch!' murmured Elsa.

'You've hit the nail on the head,' I said, turning away to hide my expression.

Elsa visibly brightened up. She had been jilted, and now she was going to show that adventuress just what she, Elsa Mackenbourg, could do. And my father loved her, as she had always known he did. Even while she had been with Juan she hadn't been able to put Raymond out of her mind. She'd never as much as mentioned the word marriage to him, and she had never bored him either, and she'd never tried . . . but by now I could endure her no longer:

'Elsa,' I said, 'go and ask Cyril from me if you could possibly stay with his mother; say you are in need of hospitality. Tomorrow morning I'll come and see him, and we'll all three discuss the situation.'

On the doorstep I added for a joke: 'You are fighting for your own future, Elsa!'

She gravely acquiesced as if there were not fifteen or twenty 'futures' in store for her, in the shape of men who would keep her. I watched her walking away in the sunshine with her mincing steps. I thought it would not be a week before my father wanted her back.

It was half past three; I imagined my father asleep in Anne's arms. I began to formulate plans one after another without pausing to think of myself. I walked up and down in my room between the door and the window, looking out from time to time at the calm sea flattening out along the beach. I calculated risks, estimated possibilities, and gradually I broke down every objection. I felt dangerously clever, and the wave of self-disgust which had swept over me from the moment I had begun to talk to Elsa now gave place to a feeling of pride in my own capabilities.

I need hardly say that all this collapsed when we went down to bathe. As soon as I saw Anne, I was overcome by remorse and did my utmost to atone for my past behaviour. I carried her bag, I rushed forward with her wrap when she came out of the water. I smothered her with attention and said the nicest things. This sudden change after my silence of the past few days was naturally a surprise to her. My father was delighted, Anne smiled at me. I thought of the words I had used in speaking of her to Elsa. How could I have said them, and how could I have put up with Elsa's nonsense? Tomorrow I would advise her to go away, saying that I had made a mistake. Everything would be as before, and, after all, why should I not pass my examination? The *baccalauréat* was sure to come in useful.

'Isn't that so?' I asked Anne. 'Isn't it useful to get one's *baccalauréat*?'

She gave me a look and burst out laughing. I followed suit, happy to see her so gay.

'You're really incredible!' she exclaimed.

I certainly was incredible, and she would have thought me even more so if she had known what I had been planning. I was dying to tell her all about it so that she could see how incredible I could be. I would have said: 'Can you imagine that I was going to make Elsa pretend to be in love with Cyril; she was to go and stay in his house, and we would have seen them passing by on his boat; strolling in the wood or along the road. Elsa looks lovely again; of course she hasn't your beauty, hers is the flamboyant kind that makes men turn round. My father wouldn't have stood it for long, he has never tolerated that a good-looking woman who had lived with him should console herself so soon, and, so to speak, before his very eyes, and above all with a man younger than himself. You understand, Anne, he would have wanted her again very quickly even though he loves you, just in order to bolster up his morale. He's very vain, or not very sure of himself, whichever way you like to put it. Elsa, under my direction, would have done all that was necessary. One day he would have been unfaithful to you and you couldn't bear that, could you? You're not one of those women who can share a man. So you would have gone away and that was exactly what I wanted. It's stupid, I know, but I was angry with you because of Bergson, of the heat; I somehow imagined . . . I daren't even tell you, it was so ridiculous and unreal. On account of my *baccalauréat* I might have quarrelled with you for ever. But it's useful to have one's *baccalauréat* all the same, isn't it . . .' 'Isn't it?' I said aloud.

'What are you trying to say?' asked Anne. 'That the *baccalauréat* is useful?'

'Yes,' I replied.

After all it was better not to tell her anything, perhaps she would not have understood. There were things Anne did not understand at all. I ran into the sea after my father and wrestled with him. Once more I was able to enjoy frolicking in the water, for I had a good conscience. Tomorrow I would change my room; I would move up to the attic with my lesson books, but Bergson would not be among them; there was no need to overdo it! For two hours every day I would concentrate in solitude on my work. I imagined myself being successful in October, and thought of my father's astonished laugh, Anne's approbation, my degree. I would be intelligent, cultured, somewhat aloof, like Anne. Perhaps I had intellectual gifts? Hadn't I been capable of producing a logical plan, despicable perhaps, but logical? And what about Elsa? I had known how to appeal to her vanity and sentimentality, and within a few minutes had managed to persuade her, when her only object in coming had been to fetch a suitcase. I felt proud of myself: I had taken stock of Elsa, found her weak spot, and carefully aimed my words. For the first time in my life I had known the intense pleasure of getting under another person's skin. It was a new experience; in the past I had always been too impulsive, and whenever I had come close to someone, it had been inadvertently. Now, when I had caught a sudden glimpse of the marvellous mechanism of human reflexes, and the power of speech, I felt sorry that I had come to it through lies. The day might come when I would love someone passionately, and would have to search warily and gently for the way to him.

3

Walking down to Cyril's villa the next morning, I felt far less sure of myself. To celebrate my recovery I had drunk too much at dinner the night before, and had been rather more than gay. I had told my father that I was going to take my degree, and would associate in future only with highbrows; that I wanted to become famous and a thorough bore. I said he must make use of every scandalous trick known to publicity in order to launch me. Roaring with laughter, we exchanged the most far-fetched ideas. Anne laughed too, but indulgently and not so loudly. When I became too extravagant, she stopped laughing altogether, but our hilarious fun had put my father into such a happy frame of mind that she said nothing. At last they went to bed, after tucking me up. I thanked them from the bottom of my heart, and asked what I would do without them. My father had no answer, but Anne seemed to have very decided views on the subject. Just as she leaned over to speak to me, I fell asleep. In the middle of the night I was sick, and my awakening the next morning was the worst I could ever remember. Still feeling very muzzy and in low spirits, I walked slowly towards the wood, but had no eyes for the sea, or for the skimming swallows.

Cyril was at the garden gate. He rushed towards me, took me in his arms, and held me tightly, talking incoherently:

'I was so worried, Darling . . . it's been so long . . . I had no idea what you were doing, or if that woman was making you unhappy . . . I've never been so miserable . . . Several times I spent all the afternoon near your creek . . . I didn't know I loved you so much . . .'

'Neither did I.'

To tell the truth, I was both surprised and touched, but I could hardly express my emotion because I felt so sick.

'How pale you are,' he said. 'From now on I'm going to look after you. I won't let you be ill-treated any more.'

I recognized Elsa's exaggerations, and asked Cyril what his mother thought of her.

'I introduced her as a friend of yours, an orphan. As a matter of fact she's very nice, she told me all about that woman. How strange it seems that, with a face like hers, she should be such an adventuress.'

'Elsa is too sensational,' I said weakly. 'But I was going to tell her . . .'

'I too, have something to tell you,' interrupted Cyril. 'Cécile, I want to marry you.'

I had a moment of panic. I absolutely had to do or say something. If only I had not felt so ill!

'I love you,' said Cyril, speaking into my hair. 'I'll give up studying law, an uncle has offered me an interesting job. I'm twenty-six. I'm not a boy any longer; I am quite serious. What do you say?'

I tried desperately to think of a non-committal, a high-sounding phrase. I did not want to marry him. I loved him, but marriage was out of the question. I had no intention of marrying anyone. I was tired.

'It's quite impossible,' I stammered. 'My father . . .'

'I'll manage your father,' said Cyril.

'Anne wouldn't approve,' I said. 'She doesn't think I'm grown-up. If she says no, my father will say the same. I'm exhausted, Cyril. All this emotion wears me out. Here's Elsa!'

She was wearing a dressing-gown, and looked fresh and radiant. I felt dull and thin. They both seemed to be overflowing with health and high spirits, which depressed me even more. She treated me as though I had come out of prison, and fussed over me, while I sat down.

'How is Raymond?' she asked. 'Does he know that I'm back?'

She had the happy smile of one who has forgiven and is full of hope. How could I tell her that my father had forgotten her, and explain to Cyril that I did not want to marry him? I shut my eyes. Cyril went to fetch some coffee. Elsa talked on and on. She obviously thought me a very subtle person in whom she could have confidence. The coffee was strong and aromatic, the sun was hot; I began to feel a little better.

'I've thought and thought, but without finding a solution,' said Elsa.

'There isn't one,' said Cyril. 'It's an infatuation; there's nothing to be done.'

'Oh yes there is!' I said. 'You just haven't any imagination.'

It flattered me to see how they hung on my words. They were ten years older than I, and they had no ideas. I said with a superior air:

'It is a question of psychology.'

I went on to explain my plan. They raised the same objections as I had done myself the day before, and I felt a particular pleasure in refuting them. I got excited all over again, in my effort to convince them that it was feasible. It only remained for me to prove to them that it ought not to be carried out, but for this I could not find any logical argument.

'I don't like that kind of intrigue,' said Cyril reluctantly. 'But if it is the only way to make you marry me, I'll do it.'

'It's not exactly Anne's fault,' I said.

'You know very well that if she stays you'll have to marry the man she chooses,' said Elsa.

Perhaps it was true. I could see Anne introducing me on my twentieth birthday to a young man with a degree to match my own, assured of a brilliant future, steady and faithful. In fact someone like Cyril himself. I began to laugh.

'Please don't laugh,' said Cyril. 'Tell me that you'll be jealous when I'm pretending to be in love with Elsa. How can you bear the thought of it for one moment? Do you love me?'

He spoke in a low voice. Elsa had gone off and discreetly left us alone. I looked at Cyril's tense brown face, his dark eyes. It gave me a strange feeling to think he loved me. I looked at his red lips, so near mine. I did not feel intellectual any longer. He came closer, our lips met and he kissed me passionately. I realized that I was more gifted for kissing a young man in the sunshine than for taking a degree. I grew away from him, gasping for breath.

'Cécile, let's stay together for ever! In the meantime I'll carry out the plan with Elsa.'

I wondered if I was right in my reckoning. As I was the instigator of the whole thing I could always stop it.

'You're full of ideas,' said Cyril with his slanting smile that lifted one side of his mouth and gave him the appearance of a handsome bandit.

And that is how I set the whole comedy in motion, against my better judgement. Sometimes I think I would blame myself less if I had been prompted that day by hatred and violence, and had not allowed myself to drift into it merely through inertia, the sun, and Cyril's kisses.

When I left the conspirators at the end of an hour, I was rather perturbed. However, there were still grounds for reassurance: my plan could misfire because my father's passion for Anne might well keep him faithful to her, besides which, neither Cyril nor Elsa could do much without my connivance. If my father showed any signs of falling into the trap, I would find some means of putting an end to the whole thing. But still it was amusing to try the plan out, and see whether my psychological judgement proved right or wrong.

What is more, Cyril was in love with me and had asked me to marry him. This was enough to make me forget everything else. If he could wait two years, to give me time to grow up, I would accept him. I could already imagine myself living with Cyril, sleeping next to him, never leaving him. Every Sunday we would go to lunch with Anne and my father, a united married couple, and sometimes perhaps include Cyril's mother, which would add a homely atmosphere to the meal.

I met Anne on the terrace on her way down to the beach to join my father. She received me with the ironical smile with which one greets those who have drunk too much the night before. I asked her what she had been going to tell me just as I fell asleep, but she only laughed and said it might make me cross. Just then my father came out of the water. He was broad and muscular, and I thought he looked wonderful. I bathed with Anne, who swam slowly with her head well out of the water so as not to wet her hair. Afterwards we three lay side by side on our stomachs in the sand, with me in the middle. We were quiet and peaceful.

Just then the boat appeared round the rocks, all sails set. My father was the first to see it.

'So Cyril couldn't hold out any longer!' he said laughing. 'Shall we forgive him, Anne? After all he's a nice boy.'

I raised my head, scenting danger.

'But what is he up to?' said my father. 'He's not coming in after all. Ah! He's not alone.'

Anne had also turned to look. The boat was going to pass right in front of us before tacking. I could make out Cyril's face. Silently I prayed that he would go away, but I could already hear my father's exclamation of surprise:

'But it's Elsa! What on earth is she doing there?'

He turned to Anne: 'That girl is extraordinary! She must already have got her claws into that poor boy and made the old lady accept her.'

But Anne was not listening; she was watching me. I saw her and hid my face in the sand to cover my shame. She put out her hand and touched my neck:

'Look at me. Are you angry with me?'

I opened my eyes. She bent over me anxiously and almost imploringly. For the first time she was treating me as a sensible, thinking person, and just on the day when . . . I groaned and jerked my head round towards my father to free myself from that hand. He was watching the boat.

'My poor child,' Anne was saying in a low voice. 'Poor little Cécile! I'm afraid it is all my fault. Perhaps I shouldn't have been so hard on you. I never wanted to hurt you, do you believe me?'

She gently stroked my hair and neck. I kept quite still. I had the same feeling as when a receding wave dragged the sand away beneath me. Neither anger nor desire had ever worked so strongly in me as my longing at that moment for utter defeat. My one wish was to give up all my plans and put myself entirely into her hands for the rest of my life. I had never before been so overcome with a sense of my utter impotence. I closed my eyes. It seemed to me that my heart stopped beating.

4

So far my father had shown no feeling other than surprise. The maid told him that Elsa had been to fetch her suitcase, but said nothing about our conversation. Being a peasant woman with a romantic turn of mind, she must have relished the various changes that had taken place in our household since she had been with us, especially in the bedrooms.

My father and Anne, in their effort to make amends, were so kind to me that at first I found it unbearable. However I soon changed my mind, for even though I had brought it on myself, I did not find it very agreeable to see Cyril and Elsa walking about arm-in-arm, showing every sign of pleasure in each other's company. I could no longer go sailing myself, but I could watch Elsa as she passed by; her hair blown by the wind, as mine used to be. It was easy enough for me to look unconcerned when we met, as we did at every corner: in the wood, in the village, and on the road. Anne would glance at me, start a new topic of conversation, and put her hand on my shoulder to comfort me. Have I ever mentioned how kind she was? Whether her kindness emanated from her intelligence, or was merely part of her detachment, I do not know, but she had an unerring instinct for the right word, and if I had really been unhappy, I could hardly have found better support.

As my father gave no signs of jealousy, I was not unduly worried, and allowed things to drift; but while it proved to me how fond he was of Anne, I felt rather annoyed that my plan had misfired. One day he and I were on our way to the post office when we passed Elsa. She pretended not to see us, and my father turned round after her with a whistle of surprise, as if she had been a stranger:

'I say! Hasn't she become a beauty!'

'Love seems to agree with her,' I remarked.

He looked rather astonished: 'You're taking it very well, I must say!'

'What can one do? They're the same age. I suppose it was inevitable.'

'If Anne hadn't come along, it wouldn't have been inevitable at all!' he said angrily. 'You don't think I'd let a boy like that snatch a woman from me without my consent?'

'All the same, age tells!' I said solemnly.

He shrugged his shoulders. On the way back I noticed he was preoccupied: perhaps he was thinking that both Cyril and Elsa were young, and that in marrying a woman of his own age, he would cease to belong to the category of men whose age does not count. I had a momentary feeling of triumph, but when I saw the tiny wrinkles at the corners of Anne's eyes, and the fine lines round her mouth, I felt ashamed of myself. It was only too easy to follow my impulses and repent afterwards.

A week went by. Cyril and Elsa, who had no idea how matters were progressing, must have been expecting me every day. I was afraid to go and see them in case they tempted me to try anything new. Every afternoon I went up to my room, ostensibly to work, but in fact I did nothing: I had found a book on Yoga, and spent my time practising various exercises. I took care to smother my laughter in case Anne should hear it. I told her I was working hard; and I pretended that my disappointment in love had made me keen to get my degree as a consolation. I hoped this would raise me in her estimation, and I even went so far as to quote Kant at table, to my father's dismay.

One afternoon I had wrapped myself in bath towels to look like a Hindu, and was sitting cross-legged staring at myself in the mirror, hoping to achieve a Yoga-like trance, when there was a knock at the door. I thought it was the maid and told her to come in.

It was Anne. For a moment she remained transfixed in the doorway, then she smiled:

'What are you playing at?'

'Yoga,' I replied. 'But it's not a game at all, it's a Hindu philosophy.'

She went to the table and took up my book. I began to be alarmed. It lay open, and every page was covered with remarks in my handwriting, such as 'Impracticable', 'Exhausting'.

'You are certainly conscientious,' she said. 'And what about that essay on Pascal? I don't see it anywhere.'

At lunch I had been talking about Pascal, implying that I had worked on a certain passage, but needless to say I had not written a word. Anne waited for me to say something, but as I did not reply she understood.

'It is your own affair if you play the fool up here instead of working, but it's quite another matter when you lie to your father and me. In any case I found it difficult to believe in your sudden intellectual activity.'

She went out of the room leaving me petrified in my bath towels. I could not understand why she had used the word 'lie'. I had spoken of Pascal because it amused me, and had mentioned an essay to give her pleasure, and now she blamed me for it. I had grown used to her new attitude towards me, and her contempt made me feel humiliated and furious. I threw off my disguise, pulled on some slacks and an old shirt and rushed out of the house. The heat was terrific, but I began to run, impelled by my anger, which was all the more violent because it was mixed with shame. I ran all the way to Cyril's villa, only stopping when I reached the door to regain my breath. In the afternoon heat the houses seemed unnaturally large and quiet, and full of secrets. I went up to Cyril's room; he had shown it to me the day we visited his mother. I opened the door. He was lying across the bed, fast asleep with his head on his arm. I stood looking at him and for the first time he appeared to me defenceless and rather touching. I called him in a low voice. He opened his eyes and sat up at once.

'You, Cécile? What's the matter?'

I signed to him not to talk so loudly. Suppose his mother were to come and find me in his room? She might think . . . anyone might think . . . I suddenly felt panic-stricken and moved towards the door.

'But where are you off to?' he cried. 'Come here, Cécile!'

He caught me by the arm and laughingly held me back. I turned round to him, and saw him grow pale, as I must have been myself. He let go my wrist, only to take me in his arms, and draw me over to the bed. The thought that it had to happen sometime flashed through my confused mind.

I stayed with him for about an hour. I was happy, but bewildered. I was used to hearing the word love bandied about, and I had often mentioned it rather crudely as one does when one is young and ignorant, but now I felt I could never talk of it again in that detached and vulgar way. Cyril, lying beside me, was talking about marrying me and how we would be together always. My silence made him uneasy. I sat up, looked at him, and called him my lover. I kissed the vein on his neck, murmuring 'Darling, darling Cyril!' I was not sure whether it was love I felt for him at that moment, I have always been fickle, and I have no wish to delude myself on this point, but just then I loved him more than myself; I would have sacrificed my life for him. He asked me when I left if I was angry with him. I laughed: how could I possibly be angry?

I walked slowly back through the pine trees; I had asked Cyril not to come with me, it would have been too risky. In any case I was afraid something might show in my face or manner. Anne was lying in front of the house on a deck chair, reading. I had a story all ready to explain where I had been, but she said nothing, she never asked questions. Then I remembered that we had quarrelled, and I sat down near her in dead silence. I remained motionless, attentive to my own breathing and the trembling of my fingers, and thinking of Cyril.

I fetched a cigarette from the table and struck a match. It went out. With shaking hands I lighted another, and although there was no wind, it went out. In exasperation I took a third, and for some reason this match assumed a vital importance; perhaps because Anne was watching me intently. Suddenly everything around me seemed to melt away and there was nothing left but the match between my fingers, the box, and Anne's eyes boring into me. My heart was beating violently. I tightened my fingers round the match and struck it, but as I bent forward my cigarette put it out. The matchbox dropped to the ground and I could feel Anne's hard, searching gaze upon me. The tension was unbearable. Then her hands were under my chin, and as she raised my face I shut my eyes tightly for fear she should read their expression and see the tears welling up. She stroked my cheek and half reluctantly let me go, as if she preferred to leave the matter in abeyance. Then she put a lighted cigarette into my mouth and returned to her book.

Perhaps the incident was symbolic. Sometimes when I am groping for a match, I find myself thinking of that strange moment when my hands no longer seemed to belong to me, and once again I remember the intensity of Anne's look, and the emptiness around me.

5

The incident I have just described was not without its aftermath. Like certain people who are very self-controlled and sure of themselves, Anne would not make concessions; and when, on the terrace, she had let me go, she was acting against her principles. She had of course guessed something, and it would have been easy enough for her to make me talk, but at the last moment she had given in to pity or indifference. It was just as hard for her to make allowances for my shortcomings, as to try to improve them, in both cases she was merely prompted by a sense of duty; in marrying my father she felt she must also take charge of me. I would have found it easier to accept her constant disapproval if she had sometimes shown exasperation, or any other feeling which went more than skin deep. One gets used to other people's faults if one does not feel it a duty to correct them. Within a few months she would have ceased to trouble about me and her indifference might then have been tempered by affection. This attitude would just have suited me. But it could never happen with her, because her sense of responsibility was too strong, especially as I was young enough to be influenced; I was malleable, though obstinate.

Therefore she had a feeling of frustration where I was concerned, she was angry with herself, and she let me know it. A few days later we were at dinner when the controversial subject of my holiday task cropped up. I let myself go, and even my father showed annoyance, but in the end it was Anne who locked me up in my room, although she had not even raised her voice during the argument. I had no idea what she had done until I tried to leave the room to fetch a glass of water. I had never been locked up in my life, and at first I panicked. I rushed over to the window, but there was no escape that way. Then I threw myself against the door so violently that I bruised my shoulder. With my teeth clenched I tried to force the lock with a pair of tweezers, but I did not want to call anyone to open it. After that I stood still in the middle of the room and collected my thoughts, and gradually I became quite calm. It was my first experience of cruelty; the thought of it lay like a stone on my heart, until it formed the central point of my resistance. I sat on my bed and began to plan my revenge. Soon I was so engrossed that several times I went to the door, and was surprised to find that I could not get out.

At six o'clock my father came to release me. I got up when he came in, and smiled at him. He looked at me in silence.

'Do you want to talk to me?' he asked.

'What about?' I said. 'You know we both have a horror of explanations that lead nowhere.'

He seemed relieved: 'But do try to be nicer to Anne, more patient.'

I was taken aback. Why should he expect me to be patient with Anne? I suddenly realized that he thought of Anne as a woman he was imposing on me, instead of the contrary. There was evidently still room for hope.

'I was horrid,' I said. 'I'll apologize to her.'

'You're not unhappy, are you?'

'Of course not!' I replied. 'And anyhow if we quarrel too often, I shall just marry a little earlier, that's all!' I knew my words would strike home.

'You mustn't look at it in that way, you're not Snow-White!

Could you bear to leave me so soon? We should only have had two years together.'

The thought was as unbearable for me as for him. I could see myself crying on his shoulder, bewailing our lost happiness. I did not want to go too far.

'I'm exaggerating, you know. With a few concessions on both sides, Anne and I will get on all right.'

'Yes,' he said. 'Of course!'

He must have thought, as I did at that moment, that the concessions would probably not be mutual, but would be on my side only.

'You see,' I told him, 'I realize very well that Anne is always right. Her life is really far more successful than ours, and has greater depth.'

He started to protest, but I went on:

'In a month or two, I shall have completely assimilated Anne's ideas, and there won't be any more stupid arguments between us. It just needs patience.'

He was obviously startled. He was not only losing a boon companion, but a slice of his past as well.

'Now don't exaggerate!' he said in a weak voice. 'I know that the kind of life you have led with me was perhaps not suitable for your age, or mine either, for that matter, but it was neither dull nor unhappy. After all, we've never been bored or depressed during the last two years, have we? There's no need to be so drastic, just because Anne's conception of life is different.'

'On the contrary,' I said firmly. 'We'll have to go even further and give up our old way of life altogether!'

'I suppose so,' said my poor father as we went downstairs together.

I made my apologies to Anne without the slightest embarrassment. She told me that I needn't have bothered; the heat must have been the cause of our dispute. I felt gay and indifferent.

I met Cyril in the wood as arranged. I told him what to do next. He listened to me with a mixture of dread and admiration. Then he took me in his arms, but I could not stay, as it was getting late. I was surprised to find that I did not want to leave him. If he had been searching for some means of attaching me to himself, he had certainly found it. I kissed him passionately. I even longed to hurt him, so that he would not be able to forget me for a single moment all the evening, and dream of me all night long. I could not bear the thought of the night without him.

6

The next morning I took my father for a walk along the road. We talked gaily of insignificant things. I suggested going back to the villa by way of the pine wood. It was exactly half past ten; I was on time. My father walked in front of me on the narrow path and pushed aside the brambles, so that I should not scratch my legs. When he stopped dead in his tracks I knew he had seen them. I went up to him; Cyril and Elsa were lying apparently asleep on the pine needles. Although they were acting entirely on my instructions, and I knew very well that they were not in love, they were nevertheless both young and beautiful, and I could not help feeling a pang of jealousy. I noticed that my father had become abnormally pale. I took him by the arm:

'Don't let's disturb them. Come on!'

He glanced once more at Elsa, who was looking particularly pretty with her red hair spread out, and a half-smile on her lips: then he turned on his heel and walked on at a brisk pace. I could hear him muttering: 'The bitch! the bitch!'

'Why do you say that? She's free, isn't she?'

'That's not the point! Did you find it very pleasant to see her in Cyril's arms?'

'I don't love him any more,' I said.

'Neither do I love Elsa,' he answered furiously. 'But it hurts all the same. After all, I've lived with her, which makes it even worse.'

I knew very well what he meant. He must have felt like dashing up to separate them and seizing his property, or what had once been his property. 'Supposing Anne were to hear you?'

'What do you mean? Well, of course, she wouldn't understand, she'd be shocked, that's normal enough! But what about you? Don't YOU understand me any more? Are you shocked too?'

How easy it was for me to steer his thoughts in the direction I wanted! It was rather frightening to know him so well.

'Of course I'm not shocked,' I said. 'But you must see things as they are: Elsa has a short memory, she finds Cyril attractive, and that's the end of it as far as you're concerned. After all, look how you behaved to her, it was unforgivable!'

'If I wanted her . . .' my father began, and then stopped short.

'You'd have no luck,' I said convincingly, as if it were the most natural thing in the world for me to discuss his chances of getting Elsa back.

'Anyhow it is out of the question,' he said in a more resigned voice.

'Of course it is!' I answered with a shrug of my shoulders, which was meant to convey that he, poor chap, was out of the running now. He said not another word until we reached the house. Then he took Anne into his arms and held her close to him. She was surprised, but gladly submitted to his embrace. I went out of the room trembling with shame.

At two o'clock I heard a soft whistle, and went down to join Cyril on the beach. We got into the boat and sailed out to sea. There was nothing in sight, no one else was out in that heat. When we were some way from the shore, he lowered the sail. So far we had hardly exchanged a word.

'This morning . . .' he began.

'Please don't talk about it!' I said.

He gently pushed me down in the boat. I could feel it swaying as we made love; the sky seemed to be falling on to us. I spoke to him, but he made no reply, there was no need. Afterwards there was the tang of salt water. We sunbathed, laughed and were happy. We had the sun and the sea, laughter and love: I wonder if we shall ever again recapture the particular flavour and brilliance of those days, heightened as they were for me by an undercurrent of fear and remorse?

The time passed quickly. I almost forgot Anne, my father, and Elsa. Through love I had entered another world: I felt dreamy, yet wide awake, peaceful, and contented. Cyril asked me if I was not afraid. I told him that I was entirely his, and he seemed satisfied that it should be so. Perhaps I had given myself to him so easily because I knew that if I had a child, he would be prepared to take the blame, and shoulder all the responsibility: this was something I could never face. For once I was thankful that my immaturity made it unlikely.

But Elsa was growing impatient. She plied me with questions. I was always afraid of being seen with her or Cyril. She lay in wait for my father at every corner, and fondly imagined that he had difficulty in keeping away from her. I was surprised that someone who hovered so precariously between love and money should get romantic ideas, and be excited by a look or movement, when such things must otherwise have been merely routine for her. The rôle she was playing evidently seemed to her the height of psychological subtlety.

Even if my father was becoming gradually obsessed with the thought of Elsa, Anne did not seem to notice it. He was more affectionate and demonstrative than ever with her, which frightened me, because I attributed it to his subconscious remorse. In three weeks we should be back in Paris, and the main thing was that nothing should happen before then. Elsa would be out of our way, and my father and Anne would get married if by then they had not changed their minds. In Paris I would have

Cyril, and just as Anne had been unable to keep us apart here, so she would find it impossible to stop me from seeing him once we were home. Cyril had a room of his own away from his mother's house. I could already picture ourselves there together, the window wide open to the wonderful pink and blue sky of Paris, pigeons cooing on the bars outside, and Cyril with me on the narrow bed.

7

A few days later my father received a message from one of our friends asking us to meet him in Saint-Raphaël for a drink. He was so pleased at the thought of escaping for a while from the unnatural seclusion in which we were living that he could hardly wait to tell us the news. I mentioned to Elsa and Cyril that we would be at the Bar du Soleil at seven o'clock and if they liked to come, they would see us there. Unfortunately, Elsa happened to know our friend, which made her all the more keen to go. I realized that there might be complications, and tried in vain to put her off.

'Charles Webb simply adores me,' she said with childlike simplicity. 'If he sees me, he's sure to make Raymond want to come back to me.'

Cyril did not care whether he went to Saint-Raphaël or not. I saw by the way he looked at me that he only wanted to be near me, and I felt proud.

At six o'clock we drove off in Anne's car. It was a huge American 'convertible', which she kept more for publicity than to suit her own taste, but it suited mine down to the ground, with all its shining gadgets. Another advantage was that we could all three sit in front, and I never feel so friendly as when I am in a car, sharing the same pleasures, and perhaps even the same death. Anne was at the wheel, as if symbolizing her future place in the family. This was the first time I had been in her car since the evening we went to Cannes.

We met Charles Webb and his wife at the Bar du Soleil. He was concerned with theatrical publicity, while his wife spent all his earnings on entertaining young men. Money was an obsession with him, he thought of nothing else in his unceasing effort to make ends meet; hence his restless impatience. He had been Elsa's lover for a long time, and she had suited him quite well, because, though very pretty, she was not particularly grasping.

His wife was a malicious woman. Anne had never met her, and I noticed that her lovely face quickly assumed the disdainful, mocking expression that was habitual to her in society. As usual Charles Webb talked all the time, now and then giving Anne an inquisitive look. He evidently wondered what she was doing with that Don Juan Raymond and his daughter. I was glad to think he would soon find out. Just then my father leant forward and said abruptly:

'I have news for you, old chap: Anne and I are getting married on the 5th of October.'

Webb looked from one to the other in amazement; his wife, who had rather a weakness for my father, seemed disconcerted.

After a pause, Webb shouted: 'Congratulations! What a splendid idea! My dear lady, you don't know what you're taking on, you are wonderful! Here, waiter! We must celebrate.'

Anne smiled quietly and indifferently. Then I saw Webb's face light up, and I did not turn round:

'Elsa! Good Heavens, it's Elsa Mackenbourg! She hasn't seen me yet. I say, Raymond, do you see how lovely that girl has grown?'

'Hasn't she!' said my father in a proprietary voice, but then he remembered and his face fell.

Anne could hardly help noticing the inflection in his voice. She turned to me with a quick movement, but before she could speak I leant towards her and said in a confidential whisper, loud enough for my father to hear:

'Anne, you're causing quite a sensation. There's a man over there who can't take his eyes off you.'

My father twisted round to look at the man in question:

'I won't have this sort of thing!' he said, taking Anne's hand.

'Aren't they sweet?' exclaimed Madame Webb, ironically. 'Charles, we really shouldn't have disturbed them; it would have been better to have invited Cécile by herself.'

'She wouldn't have come,' I said unhesitatingly.

'Why not? Are you in love with one of the fishermen?'

She had once seen me in conversation with a bus conductor, and ever since had treated me as though I had lost caste.

'Why yes, of course!' I said with an effort to appear gay.

'And do you go out fishing a lot?'

She thought she was being funny, which made it even worse. I was beginning to get angry, but did not know what to answer without being too offensive. There was dead silence. Anne's voice interposed quietly:

'Raymond, would you mind asking the waiter to bring me a straw to drink my orange juice?'

Charles Webb began to talk feverishly about refreshing drinks. Anne gave me a look of entreaty. We all decided to dine together as though we had narrowly escaped a scene.

At dinner I drank far too much. I wanted to forget Anne's anxious expression when she looked at my father, and the hint of gratitude in her eyes whenever they rested on me. Every time Madame Webb made a dig at me I gave her an ingratiating smile. This seemed to upset her, and she soon became openly aggressive. Anne signed to me to keep quiet, she had a horror of scenes in public, and Madame Webb seemed to be on the point of creating one. For my part I was used to them. Among our associates they were frequent, so I was not disturbed by the prospect.

After dinner we went to another bar. Soon Elsa and Cyril turned up. Elsa was talking very loudly as she entered the room followed by poor Cyril. I thought she was behaving badly, but she was pretty enough to carry it off.

'Who's that puppy she's with?' asked Charles Webb. 'He's rather young, isn't he?'

'It's love that keeps him young!' simpered his wife.

'Don't you believe it!' said my father. 'It's just an infatuation.'

I had my eyes on Anne. She was watching Elsa in the calm, detached way she looked at very young women, or at the mannequins parading her collection. For a moment I admired her passionately for showing no trace of jealousy or spite, but how could she be jealous, I wondered, when she herself was a hundred times more beautiful and intelligent than Elsa? As I was very drunk, I told her so. She looked at me curiously:

'Do you really think I am more beautiful than Elsa?'

'Of course!'

'That is always pleasant to hear, but you are drinking too much. Give me your glass. I hope it doesn't upset you to see Cyril here? Anyway he seems bored to death.'

'He's my lover,' I said with gay abandon.

'You are quite drunk. Fortunately it's time to go home.'

It was a relief to part from the Webbs. I found it difficult to say goodbye politely. My father drove, and my head lolled on to Anne's shoulder.

I began to reflect how much I preferred her to the people we usually saw, that she was infinitely superior to them in every way. My father said very little, perhaps he was thinking of Elsa.

'Is she sleeping?' he asked Anne.

'As peacefully as a baby. She didn't behave badly on the whole, did she?'

They were silent for a while, then I heard his voice again:
'Anne, I love you; only you. Do you believe me?'
'Don't tell me so often, it frightens me.'
'Give me your hand.'

I almost sat up to protest: 'For heaven's sake, not on the Corniche!', but I was too drunk, and half asleep. Besides there was Anne's perfume, the sea breeze in my hair, the tiny graze on my shoulder which was a reminder of Cyril; all these reasons to be happy and keep quiet. I thought of Elsa and Cyril setting off on the motor cycle which had been a birthday present from his mother. I felt so sorry for them that I almost cried. Anne's car was made for sleeping, so well sprung, not noisy like a motor bike. I thought of Madame Webb lying awake at night. No doubt at her age I would also have to pay someone to love me, because love is the most wonderful thing in the world. What does the price matter? The important thing was not to become embittered and jealous, as she was of Elsa and Anne. I began to laugh softly to myself. Anne moved her shoulder to make a comfortable hollow for me. 'Go to sleep,' she ordered. I went to sleep.

8

The next morning I woke up feeling perfectly well except for a slight ache in my neck. My bed was flooded with sunshine as it was every morning. I threw back the sheets and exposed my bare back to the sun. It was warm and comforting, and seemed to penetrate my very bones. I decided to spend the morning like that, without moving.

In my mind I went over the events of the evening before. I remembered telling Anne that Cyril was my lover. It amused me to think that one can tell the truth when one is drunk and nobody will believe it. I thought about Madame Webb. I was used to that sort of woman: in her milieu and at her age they often become odious through their self-indulgence; Anne's calm dignity had shown her up as even more idiotic and boring than usual. It was only to be expected; I could not imagine anyone among my father's friends who would for a moment bear comparison with Anne. In order to be able to face an evening with people like that, one had either to be rather drunk, or be on intimate terms with one or other of them. For my father it was more simple: Charles Webb and he were libertines: 'Guess whom I'm taking out tonight? The Mars girl, the one in Saurel's latest film.' My father would laugh, and clap him on the back: 'Lucky man! She's almost as pretty as Élise.' Undergraduate talk, but I liked their enthusiasm.

Then there were interminable evenings on café terraces, and

Lombard's tales of woe: 'She was the only one I ever loved, Raymond! Do you remember that spring before she left me? It's stupid for a man to devote his whole life to one woman.' This was another side of life.

Anne's friends probably never talked about themselves, perhaps they did not indulge in such adventures. Or if they spoke of them, it must be with an apologetic laugh. Already I almost shared Anne's condescending attitude towards our friends: it was catching. On the other hand, by the age of thirty, I could imagine myself being more like them than like Anne, and by then her silence, indifference and reserve might suffocate me. There was a knock at the door. I quickly put on my pyjama top and called 'Come in!' Anne stood there, carefully holding a cup.

'I thought you might like some coffee. How do you feel this morning?'

'Very well,' I answered. 'I'm afraid I was a bit tipsy last night.'

'As you are each time you go out,' she began to laugh. 'But I must say, you were amusing. It was such a tedious evening.'

I had forgotten the sun, and even my coffee. When I was talking to Anne, I was completely absorbed; I did not think of myself, and yet she was the only one who made me question my motives. Through her I lived more intensely.

'Cécile, do you find people like the Webbs and the Dupuis entertaining?'

'Well, they usually behave abominably, but they are funny.'

She was watching a fly on the floor. Anne's eyelids were long and heavy; it was easy for her to look condescending.

'Don't you ever realize how monotonous and dull their conversation is? Don't those endless stories about girls, contracts and parties bore you?'

'I'm afraid,' I answered, 'that after ten years of convent life their lack of morals fascinates me.'

I did not dare to add that I also liked it.

'You left two years ago,' she said. 'It's not anything one can reason about, neither is it a question of morals; it has something to do with one's sensibility, a sixth sense.'

I supposed I hadn't got it. I saw clearly that I was lacking in this respect.

'Anne,' I asked abruptly, 'do you think I am intelligent?'

She began to laugh, surprised at the directness of my question.

'Of course you are! Why do you ask?'

'If I were an idiot, you'd say just the same thing,' I sighed. 'I so often find your superiority overpowering.'

'It's just a question of age,' she answered. 'It would be a sad thing if I didn't feel a little more self-assured than you.'

She laughed. I was annoyed:

'It wouldn't necessarily be a bad thing.'

'It would be a catastrophe,' she said.

She suddenly dropped her bantering tone and looked me straight in the face. I at once felt ill-at-ease, and began to fidget. Even today I cannot get used to people who stare at you while they are talking, or come very close to make quite sure that you are listening. My only thought then is to escape from such proximity. I go on saying 'Yes', while gradually edging away; their insistence and indiscretion enrage me. What right have they to try to corner me? Fortunately, Anne did not resort to these tactics, but merely kept her eyes fixed on me, so that I could no longer continue to talk in the light-hearted vein I usually affected.

'Do you know how men like Webb end up?'

I thought: 'And men like my father.'

'In the river,' I answered flippantly.

'A time comes when they are no longer attractive or in good form. They can't drink any more, and they still hanker after women, only then they have to pay and make compromises in order to escape from their loneliness: they have become just figures of fun. They grow sentimental and hard to please. I have seen many who have gone the same way.'

'Poor Webb!' I said.

I was impressed. So that was the fate in store for my father? Or at least the fate from which Anne was saving him.

'You never thought of that, did you?' said Anne, with a little smile of commiseration. 'You don't think much about the future, do you? That is the privilege of youth.'

'Please don't throw my youth at me like that! I use it neither as an excuse, nor as a privilege. I just don't attach any importance to it.'

'To what do you attach importance? To your peace of mind? Your independence?'

I dreaded conversations of this sort, especially with Anne.

'To nothing at all,' I said. 'You know I hardly ever think.'

'You and your father irritate me at times: "You haven't given it a thought . . . you're not up to much . . . you don't know." Are you satisfied to be like that?'

'I'm not satisfied with myself. I don't like myself, and I don't try to. At moments you force me to complicate my life, and I almost hate you for it.'

She began to hum to herself with a thoughtful expression. I recognized the tune, but did not know what it was:

'What's the name of that song, Anne? It gets on my nerves.'

'I don't know,' she smiled again, looking rather discouraged. 'Stay in bed and rest, I'll continue my research on the family intellect somewhere else.'

I thought it was easy enough for my father. I could just imagine him saying 'I'm not thinking of anything special because I love you, Anne.' However intelligent she was, Anne would accept this as a valid excuse. I gave myself a good stretch and lay down on my pillow. Anne was dramatizing the situation: in twenty-five years my father would be an amiable sexagenarian with white hair, rather addicted to whisky and highly-coloured reminiscences. We would go out together; it would be my turn to tell him my adventures, and his to advise me. I realized that in my mind I was excluding Anne from our future: I did not see how she could fit in. Amidst the turmoil of our flat, which was sometimes bare, at others full of flowers, the stage for many and varied scenes, often cluttered up with luggage, I somehow could not envisage the introduction of order, the peace and quiet, the feeling of harmony that Anne brought with her everywhere she went, as if they were the most precious gifts. I dreaded being bored to death; although I was less apprehensive of her influence since my love for Cyril had liberated me from many of my fears. I feared boredom and tranquillity more than anything. In order to achieve serenity, my father and I had to have excitement, and this Anne was not prepared to admit.

9

I have spoken a great deal about Anne and myself, and very little of my father. Yet he has played the most important part in this story, and my feelings for him have been deeper and more stable than for anyone else. I know him too well, and feel too close to him to talk easily of him, and it is he above all others whom I wish to justify and present in a good light. He was neither vain nor selfish, but incurably frivolous. I could not call him irresponsible or incapable of deep feelings. His love for me is not to be taken lightly or regarded merely as a parental habit. He could suffer more through me than through anyone else, and for my part I was nearer to despair the day he turned away as if abandoning me than I had ever been in my life. I was always more important to him than his love affairs. On certain evenings, by taking me home, he must have missed what his friend Webb would have called 'great opportunities'. On the other hand, I cannot deny that he was unfaithful and would always take the easiest way. He never reflected, and tried to give everything a physiological explanation which he called being rational: 'You think yourself hateful? Sleep more and drink less!' It was the same when at times he had a violent desire for a particular woman. He never thought of repressing it, or trying to elevate it into a complex sentiment. He was a materialist, but kind and understanding and had a touch of delicacy. His desire for Elsa disturbed him, but not in the way one might expect. He did not say to himself: 'I want to be unfaithful to Anne, therefore I love her less,' but 'This need for Elsa is a nuisance, I must get over it quickly or it might cause complications with Anne.' Moreover he loved and admired Anne. She was a change from the stupid and frivolous women he had consorted with in recent years. She satisfied his vanity, his sensuality and his sensibility, for she understood him, and offered her intelligence and experience to supplement his. But I do not believe he realized how deeply she cared for him. He thought of her as the ideal mistress and an ideal mother for me, but I do not think he visualized her as the ideal wife for himself, with all this implied. I am sure that in Cyril's and in Anne's eyes he was like me, abnormal, so to speak; but although he considered his life banal, he put all his vitality into it and made it exciting.

I was not thinking of him when I formed the project of shutting Anne out of our lives; I knew he would console himself as he always did: a clean break with Anne would in the long run be less painful than living a well-regulated life as her husband. What really destroyed him, as it did me, was being subjected to fixed habits. We were of the same race; sometimes I thought we belonged to the pure and beautiful race of nomads, and at others to the poor withered breed of hedonists.

At that moment he was suffering, or at least he was feeling exasperated: Elsa had become the symbol of his past life and of youth, above all his own youth. I knew he was dying to say to Anne: 'Dearest, let me go for just one day; I must prove to myself with Elsa's help that I'm not an old fogey.' But that was impossible; not because Anne was jealous, or too virtuous to discuss such matters, but because she had made up her mind to live with him on her own terms. She was determined to put an end to the era of frivolity and debauch and to stop him behaving like a schoolboy. She was entrusting her life to him and in future he must behave well and not be a slave to his caprices. One could not blame Anne: hers was a perfectly normal and sensible point of view, but it did not prevent my father from wanting Elsa – from desiring her more and more as time passed and his feeling of frustration increased.

At that moment I have no doubt that I could have arranged everything. I had only to tell Elsa to go and meet him and resume their former relations, and I could easily have persuaded Anne to go with me to Nice on some pretext. On our return we would have found my father relaxed, and filled with a new taste for legalized affections, or rather, those shortly to become legalized. But Anne could not have borne the idea of having been merely a mistress like the others. How difficult she made life for us through the high esteem in which she held herself!

But I said nothing to Elsa, neither did I ask Anne to go to Nice with me. I wanted my father's desire to fester in him, so that in the end he would give himself away. I could not bear the contempt with which Anne treated our past life, her disdain for what had been our happiness. I had no wish to humiliate her, but only to force her to accept our way of life. For this it was necessary that she should discover his infidelity, and should see it objectively as a passing fancy, not as an attack on her personal dignity. If at all cost she wished to be in the right, she must allow us to be in the wrong.

I even pretended not to notice my father's plight. On no account could I become his accomplice by speaking to Elsa for him, or getting Anne out of the way. I had to pretend to look upon Anne and his love for her as sacred, and I must admit it was not difficult for me. The idea that he could be unfaithful and defy her filled me with terror and a vague admiration.

In the meanwhile we had many happy days. I made use of every occasion to further my father's interest in Elsa. The sight of Anne's face no longer filled me with remorse. I sometimes imagined that she would accept everything, and that we would be able to live a life that suited us all three equally well. I often saw Cyril, and we made love in secret. The scent of the pines, and the sound of the sea added to the enchantment. He began to torment himself; he hated the rôle I had forced upon him, and only continued with it because I made him believe it was necessary for our love. All this involved a great deal of deceit, and much had to be concealed, but it did not cost me much effort to tell a few lies, and after all, I alone controlled, and was the sole judge of my actions.

I will pass quickly over this period, for I am afraid that if I look at it closely, I shall revive memories that are too painful. Already I feel overwhelmed as I think of Anne's happy laugh, of her kindness to me. My conscience troubles me so much at those moments that I am obliged to resort to some expedient like lighting a cigarette, putting on a record, or telephoning to a friend. Then gradually I begin to think of something else. But I do not like having to take refuge in forgetfulness and frivolity instead of facing my memories and fighting them.

10

Destiny sometimes assumes strange forms. That summer it appeared in the guise of Elsa, a mediocre person, but with a pretty face. She had an extraordinary laugh, sudden and infectious, which only rather stupid people possess.

I soon noticed the effect of this laugh on my father. I told her to make the utmost use of it whenever we 'surprised' her with Cyril. My orders were: 'When you hear me coming with my father, say nothing, just laugh.' And at the sound of that laugh a look of fury would come into my father's face. My rôle of stage manager continued to be exciting. I never missed my mark, for when we saw Cyril and Elsa openly showing signs of an imaginary relationship my father and I both grew pale with the violence of our feelings. The sight of Cyril bending over Elsa made my heart ache. I would have given anything in that world to stop them, forgetting that it was I who had planned it.

Apart from these incidents and filling our daily life were Anne's confidence, gentleness and (I hate to use the word) happiness. She was nearer to happiness than I had ever seen her since she had been at our mercy, egoists that we were. She was far removed from our violent desires and my base little schemes. I had counted on her aloofness and instinctive pride preventing her from making any special effort to attach my father to her, and that she would rely on looking beautiful, and being her intelligent, loving self.

I began to feel sorry for her, and pity is an agreeable sentiment, moving, like military music.

One fine morning the maid, in great excitement, handed me a note from Elsa: 'All is well. Come!' I had an impression of imminent catastrophe: I hate final scenes. I met Elsa on the beach, looking triumphant.

'At last I managed to speak to your father, just an hour ago.'

'What did he say?'

'He told me he was very sorry for what had happened, that he had behaved like a cad. It's the truth, isn't it?'

I thought it best to agree.

'Then he paid me compliments in the way only he can, you know, rather detached, in a low voice, as if at the same time it hurt him.'

I interrupted her: 'What was he leading up to?'

'Well, nothing. Oh yes, he asked me to have tea with him in the village to show there was no ill-feeling, and that I was broad-minded. Shall I go?'

My father's views on the broad-mindedness of red-haired girls were a treat. I felt like saying that it had nothing to do with me. Then I realized that she held me responsible for her success. Rightly or wrongly, it irritated me. I felt trapped.

'I don't know, Elsa. That depends on you. You always ask me what you should do, one might almost believe that it was I who forced you . . .'

'But it was you,' she said. 'It's entirely through you that . . .'

The admiration in her voice suddenly frightened me:

'Go if you want to, but for heaven's sake, don't say any more about it!'

'But Cécile, isn't the whole idea to free him from that woman's clutches?'

I fled. Let my father do as he wished, and Anne must deal with it as best she could. Anyhow I was on my way to meet

Cyril. It seemed to me that love was the only remedy for the haunting fear I felt.

Cyril took me in his arms without a word. Once I was with him, everything became quite simple. Later, lying beside him, I told him that I hated myself. I smiled as I said it because although I meant it, there was no pain, only a pleasant resignation. He did not take me seriously:

'What does it matter? I love you so much that I shall make you feel as I do.'

All through our midday meal I thought of his words: 'I love you so much.' That is why, although I have tried hard, I cannot remember much about that lunch. Anne was wearing a mauve dress, as mauve as the shadows under her eyes; the colour of her eyes themselves. My father laughed, and was evidently well pleased with himself: everything was going well for him. During dessert he announced that he had some shopping to do in the village that afternoon. I smiled to myself. I was tired of the whole thing, and felt fatalistic about it. My one desire was to have a swim.

At four o'clock I went down to the beach. I saw my father on the terrace about to leave for the village; I did not speak, not even to warn him to be careful.

The water was soft and warm. Anne did not appear. I supposed she was busy in her room designing her next collection, and meanwhile my father was making the most of his time with Elsa. After two hours, when I was tired of sunbathing, I went up to the terrace and sitting down in a chair, opened a newspaper.

At that moment Anne appeared from the direction of the wood. She was running, clumsily, heavily, her elbows close to her sides. I had a sudden, ghastly impression of an old woman running towards me, and that she was about to fall down. I did not move; she disappeared behind the house near the garage. In a flash I understood, and I too began running to catch her.

She was already in her car starting it up. I rushed over and clutched at the door.

'Anne,' I cried. 'Don't go, it's all a mistake, it's my fault. I'll explain everything.'

She paid no attention to me, but bent to take the brake off.

'Anne, we need you!'

She straightened up, and I saw that her face was distorted; she was crying. Then I realized that I had attacked a living, sensitive creature, not just an entity. She too must once have been a rather secretive little girl, then an adolescent, and after that a woman. Now she was forty, and all alone. She loved a man, and had hoped to spend ten or twenty happy years with him. As for me . . . that poor miserable face was my work. I was petrified; I trembled all over as I leant against the door.

'You have no need of anyone,' she murmured. 'Neither you nor he.'

The engine was running. I was desperate, she couldn't go like that!

'Forgive me! I beg you . . .'

'Forgive you? What for?'

The tears were streaming down her face. She did not seem to notice them.

'My poor child!'

She laid her hand against my cheek for a moment, then drove away. I saw her car disappearing round the side of the house. I was irretrievably lost. It had all happened so quickly. I thought of her face.

I heard steps behind me: it was my father. He had taken the time to remove the imprint of Elsa's lipstick from his face, and brush the pine needles from his suit. I turned round and threw myself on him.

'You beast!'

I began to sob.

'But what's the matter? Where is Anne? Cécile, tell me, Cécile!'

II

We did not meet again until dinner. Both of us were nervous at being suddenly alone together, and neither he nor I had any appetite. We realized it was necessary to get Anne back. I could not bear to think of the look of horror on her face before she left, of her distress and my own responsibility. All my cunning manoeuvres and carefully laid plans were forgotten. I was thrown completely off my balance, and I could see from his expression that my father felt the same.

'Do you think,' he said, 'that she'll stay away from us for long?'

'I expect she's gone to Paris,' I said.

'Paris,' murmured my father in a dreamy voice.

'Perhaps we shall never see her again.'

He seemed at a loss for words, and took my hand across the table.

'You must be terribly angry with me. I don't know what came over me. On the way back through the woods I kissed Elsa, and just at that moment Anne must have arrived.'

I was not listening. The figures of Elsa and my father embracing under the pines seemed theatrical and unreal to me, and I could not visualize them. The only vivid memory of that day was my last glimpse of Anne's face with its look of grief and betrayal.

I took a cigarette from my father's packet and lit it. Smoking during meals was a thing Anne could not bear.

I smiled at my father:

'I understand very well, it's not your fault. It was a momentary lapse, as they say. But we must get Anne to forgive us, or rather you.'

'What shall we do?' he asked me.

He looked far from well. I felt sorry for him and for myself too. After all, what was Anne up to, leaving us in the lurch like that, making us suffer for one moment of folly? Hadn't she a duty towards us?

'Let's write to her,' I said. 'And ask her forgiveness.'

'What a wonderful idea,' said my father.

At last he had found some means of escape from the stupor and remorse of the past three hours. Without waiting to finish our meal, we pushed back the cloth, my father went to fetch a lamp, pens, and some notepaper; we sat down opposite each other, almost smiling because our preparations had made Anne's return seem probable. A bat was circling round outside the window. My father started writing.

An unbearable feeling of disgust and horror rises in me when I think of the letters full of fine sentiments we wrote that evening, sitting under the lamp like two awkward schoolchildren, applying ourselves in silence to the impossible task of getting Anne back. However we managed to produce two works of art, full of excuses, love, and repentance. When I had finished, I felt almost certain that Anne would not be able to resist us, and that a reconciliation was imminent. I could already imagine the scene as she forgave us, it would take place in our drawing-room in Paris, Anne would come in and . . .

At that moment the telephone rang. It was ten o'clock. We exchanged a look of astonishment which soon turned to hope; it was Anne telephoning to say she forgave us and was returning. My father bounded to the telephone and called 'Hello' in a voice full of joy.

Then he said nothing but 'Yes, yes, where is that? yes' in an almost inaudible whisper. I got up, shaken by fear. My father passed his hand over his face with a mechanical gesture. At length he gently replaced the receiver and turned to me:

'She has had an accident,' he said. 'On the road to Estérel. It took them some time to discover her address. They telephoned to Paris and got our number from there.'

He went on in the same flat voice, and I dared not interrupt:

'The accident happened at the most dangerous spot. There have been many at that place, it seems. The car fell down fifty metres. It would have been a miracle if she had escaped.'

The rest of that night I remember as if it had been a nightmare: the road surging up under the headlights, my father's stony face, the door of the clinic. My father would not let me see her. I sat on a bench in the waiting-room staring at a lithograph of Venice. I thought of nothing. A nurse told me that this was the sixth accident at that place since the beginning of the summer. My father did not come back.

Then I thought that once again by her death Anne had proved herself different from us. If we had wanted to commit suicide, even supposing we had the courage, it would have been with a bullet in the head, leaving an explanatory note destined to trouble the sleep of those who were responsible. But Anne had made us the magnificent present of giving us the chance to believe in an accident. A dangerous place on the road, a car that easily lost balance. It was a gift that we would soon be weak enough to accept. In any case it is a romantic idea of mine to call it suicide. Can one commit suicide on account of people like my father and myself, people who have no need of anybody, living or dead? My father and I never spoke of it as anything but an accident.

The next day we returned to the house at about three o'clock in the afternoon. Elsa and Cyril were waiting for us, sitting on the steps. They seemed like two comic, forgotten characters; neither of them had known Anne, or loved her. There they were with their little love affairs, their good looks, and their embarrassment. Cyril came up to me and put his hand on my arm. I looked at him: I had never loved him. I had found him gentle and attractive. I had loved the pleasure he gave me, but I did not need him. I was going away, leaving behind me the house, the garden, and that summer. My father was with me; he took my arm and we went indoors.

In the house were Anne's jacket, her flowers, her room, her scent. My father closed the shutters, took a bottle out of the refrigerator and fetched two glasses. It was the only remedy to hand. Our letters of excuse still lay on the table. I pushed them off and they floated to the floor. My father, who was coming towards me holding a full glass, hesitated, then, avoided them. I found it symbolical. I took my glass and drained it in one gulp. The room was in half darkness, I saw my father's shadow on the window. The sea was beating on the shore.

12

The funeral took place in Paris on a fine day. There was the usual curious crowd dressed in black. My father and I shook hands with Anne's elderly relations. I looked at them with interest: they would probably have come to tea with us once a year. People commiserated with my father. Webb must have spread the news of his intended marriage. I saw that Cyril was looking for me after the service, but I avoided him. The resentment I felt towards him was quite unjustified, but I could not help it. Everyone was deploring the dreadful and senseless event, and as I was still rather doubtful whether it had been an accident, I was relieved.

In the car on the way back, my father took my hand and held it tightly. I thought: 'Now we have only each other, we are alone and unhappy,' and for the first time I cried. My tears were some comfort, they were not at all like the terrible emptiness I had felt in the clinic in front of the picture of Venice. My father gave me his handkerchief without a word, his face was ravaged.

For a month we lived like a widower and an orphan, eating all our meals together and staying at home. Sometimes we spoke of Anne: 'Do you remember the day when . . . ?' We chose our words with care, and averted our eyes for fear we might hurt each other, or that something irreparable would come between us. Our discretion and restraint brought their own recompense. Soon we could speak of Anne in a normal way as of a person dear to us, with whom we could have been happy, but whom God had called to Himself. God instead of chance. We did not believe in God. In these circumstances we were thankful to believe in fate.

Then one day at a friend's house I met a young man I liked and who liked me. For a week I went out with him constantly, and my father, who could not bear to be alone, followed my example with an ambitious young woman. Life began to take its old course, as it was bound to. When my father and I were alone together we joked, and discussed our latest conquests. He must suspect that my friendship with Philippe is not platonic, and I know very well that his new friend is costing him too much money. But we are happy. Winter is drawing to an end; we shall not rent the same villa again, but another one, near Juan-les-Pins.

Only when I am in bed, at dawn, listening to the cars passing below in the streets of Paris, my memory betrays me: that summer returns to me with all its memories. Anne, Anne, I repeat over and over again softly in the darkness. Then something rises in me that I welcome by name, with closed eyes: Bonjour tristesse!

PENGUIN ESSENTIALS

COLD COMFORT FARM/STELLA GIBBONS

'We are not like other folk, maybe, but there have always been Starkadders at Cold Comfort Farm...'

Sensible, sophisticated Flora Poste has been expensively educated to do everything but earn a living. When she is orphaned at twenty, she decides her only option is to descend on relatives – the doomed Starkadders at the aptly named Cold Comfort Farm. There is Judith in a scarlet shawl, heaving with remorse for an unspoken wickedness; raving old Ada Doom, who once saw something nasty in the woodshed; lustful Seth and despairing Reuben, Judith's two sons; and there is Amos, preaching fire and damnation to one and all. As the sukebind flowers, Flora takes each of the family in hand and brings order to their chaos.

Cold Comfort Farm is a sharp and clever parody of the melodramatic and rural novel.

'Very probably the funniest book ever written' *Sunday Times*

GOODBYE TO ALL THAT/ROBERT GRAVES

'There has been a lot of fighting hereabouts. The trenches have made themselves rather than been made, and run inconsequently in and out of the big thirty-foot high stacks of bricks; it is most confusing. The parapet of a trench which we don't occupy is built up with ammunition boxes and corpses . . .'

In one of the most honest and candid self-portraits ever committed to paper, Robert Graves tells the extraordinary story of his experiences as a young officer in the First World War. He describes life in the trenches in vivid, raw detail, how the dehumanizing horrors he witnessed left him shell-shocked. They were to haunt him for the rest of his life.

'One of the classic accounts of the Western Front' *The Times*

PENGUIN ESSENTIALS

STEPPENWOLF/HERMANN HESSE

'The unhappiness that I need and long for . . . is of the kind that will let me suffer with eagerness and die with lust. That is the unhappiness, or happiness, that I am waiting for.'

Alienated from society, Harry Haller is the Steppenwolf, wild, strange and shy. His despair and desire for death draw him into an enchanted, Faustian underworld. Through a series of shadowy encounters – romantic, freakish and savage by turn – Haller begins to rediscover the lost dreams of his youth.

Adopted by the Sixties counterculture, *Steppenwolf* captured the mood of a disaffected generation that was beginning to question everything.

'The gripping and fascinating story of disease in a man's soul, and a savage indictment of bourgeois society' *New York Times*

LOLITA/VLADIMIR NABOKOV

'Lolita, light of my life, fire of my loins. My sin, my soul. Lo-lee-ta: the tip of my tongue taking a trip of three steps down the palate to tap, at three, on the teeth. Lo. Lee. Ta.'

Humbert Humbert is a middle-aged, frustrated college professor. In love with his landlady's twelve-year-old daughter Lolita, he'll do anything to possess her. Unable and unwilling to stop himself, he is prepared to commit any crime to get what he wants.

Is he in love or insane? A silver-tongued poet or a pervert? A tortured soul or a monster? Or is he all of these?

'You read Lolita sprawling limply in your chair, ravished, overcome, nodding scandalized assent' Martin Amis, *Observer*

PENGUIN ESSENTIALS

WIDE SARGASSO SEA/JEAN RHYS

'There is no looking glass here and I don't know what I am like now… Now they have taken everything away. What am I doing in this place and who am I?'

If Antoinette Cosway, a spirited Creole heiress, could have foreseen the terrible future that awaited her, she would not have married the young Englishman. Initially drawn to her beauty and sensuality, he becomes increasingly frustrated by his inability to reach into her soul. He forces Antoinette to conform to his rigid Victorian ideals, unaware that in taking away her identity he is destroying a part of himself as well as pushing her towards madness.

Set against the lush backdrop of 1830s Jamaica, Jean Rhys's powerful, haunting masterpiece was inspired by her fascination with the first Mrs Rochester, the mad wife in Charlotte Brontë's *Jane Eyre*.

'Compelling, painful and exquisite' *Guardian*

HELL'S ANGELS/HUNTER S. THOMPSON

'A phalanx of motorcycles came roaring over the hill from the west… the noise was like a landslide, or a wing of bombers passing over. Even knowing the Angels I couldn't quite handle what I was seeing. It was like Genghis Khan, Morgan's Raiders, the Wild One and the Rape of Nanking all at once.'

In September, 1964 a cavalcade of motorbikes ripped through the city of Monterey, California. It was a trip destined to make Hell's Angels household names across America, infamous for their violent, drunken rampages and feared for the destruction left in their wake.

Enter Hunter S. Thompson, the master of counter-culture journalism who alone had the ability and stature to ride with the Angels on their terms. In this brilliant and hair-raising expose, he journeys with the last outlaws of the American frontier.

A mixture of journalism, story-telling and sheer bravado, *Hell's Angels* is Hunter S. Thompson at full throttle.

'The maverick voice of American counterculture' *Guardian*

PENGUIN ESSENTIALS

EVA LUNA/ISABEL ALLENDE

'My name is Eva, which means "life", according to a book of names my mother consulted. I was born in the back room of a shadowy house, and grew up amidst ancient furniture, books in Latin, and human mummies, but none of those things made me melancholy, because I came into the world with a breath of the jungle in my memory.'

Isabel Allende tells the sweet and sinister story of an orphan who beguiles the world with her astonishing visions, triumphing over the worst of adversity and bringing light to a dark place.

'A heartfelt novel, powerful enough to make a dictator cry' *Evening Standard*

OUT OF AFRICA/KAREN BLIXEN

'I had a farm in Africa, at the foot of the Ngong Hills . . . Up in this high air you breathed easily . . . you woke up in the morning and thought: Here I am, where I ought to be.'

From the moment Karen Blixen arrived in Kenya in 1914 to manage a coffee plantation, her heart belonged to Africa. Drawn to the intense colours and ravishing landscapes, Blixen spent her happiest years on the farm, and her experiences and friendships with the people around her are vividly recalled in these memoirs.

Out of Africa is the story of a remarkable and unconventional woman, and of a way of life that has vanished for ever.

'A compelling story of passion and a movingly poetic tribute to a lost land' *The Times*

PENGUIN ESSENTIALS

ON THE ROAD/JACK KEROUAC

'What's your road, man? — holyboy road, madman road, rainbow road, guppy road, any road. It's an anywhere road for anybody anyhow.'

Sal Paradise, young and innocent, joins the slightly crazed Dean Moriarty on a breathless, exuberant ride back and forth across the United States. Their hedonistic search for release or fulfilment through drink, sex, drugs and jazz becomes an exploration of personal freedom, a test of the limits of the American Dream.

A brilliant blend of fiction and autobiography, Jack Kerouac's exhilarating novel defined the new 'Beat' generation and became the bible of the counter culture.

'Pop writing at its best. It changed the way I saw the world, making me yearn for fresh experience' Hanif Kureishi, *Independent on Sunday*

LADY CHATTERLEY'S LOVER/D.H. LAWRENCE

'Connie was aware, however, of a growing restlessness … It thrilled inside her body, in her womb, somewhere, till she felt she must jump into water and swim to get away from it; a mad restlessness. It made her heart beat violently for no reason …'

Lady Constance Chatterley is trapped in a loveless marriage to a man who is impotent. Oppressed by her dreary life, she is drawn to Mellors the gamekeeper. Breaking out against the constraints of society she yields to her instinctive desire for him and discovers the transforming power of physical love which leads them both towards fulfilment.

Banned for many years for its frank depiction of sex, *Lady Chatterley's Lover* was first published by Penguin in 1960 and was at the centre of a sensational obscenity trial at the Old Bailey. D. H. Lawrence himself called it 'the most improper novel in the world'.

'No one ever wrote better about the power struggles of sex and love' Doris Lessing

PENGUIN ESSENTIALS

A CLOCKWORK ORANGE/ANTHONY BURGESS

'What we were after was lashings of ultraviolence'

In this nightmare vision of youth in revolt, fifteen-year-old Alex and his friends set out on a diabolical orgy of robbery, rape, torture and murder. Alex is jailed for his teenage delinquency and the State tries to reform him – but at what cost?

Social prophecy? Black comedy? Study of freewill? *A Clockwork Orange* is all of these. It is also a dazzling experiment in language, as Burgess creates a new language – 'nadsat', the teenage slang of a not-too-distant future.

'A gruesomely witty cautionary tale' *Time*

BREAKFAST AT TIFFANY'S/TRUMAN CAPOTE

'What I've found does the most good is just to get into a taxi and go to Tiffany's. It calms me down right away, the quietness and the proud look of it; nothing very bad could happen to you there, not with those kind men in their nice suits...'

Meet Holly Golightly – a free spirited, lop-sided romantic girl about town. With her tousled blond hair and upturned nose, dark glasses and chic black dresses, Holly is a style sensation wherever she goes. Her apartment rocks to Martini-soaked parties and she plays hostess to millionaires and gangsters alike. Yet Holly never loses sight of her ultimate dream – to find a real life place like Tiffany's that makes her feel at home.

Full of sharp wit and exuberant, larger-than-life characters which vividly capture the restless, madcap era of 1940s New York, *Breakfast at Tiffany's* will make you fall in love, perhaps for the first time, with a book.

'The most romantic story ever written' Alex James, *Guardian*

PENGUIN ESSENTIALS

MY FAMILY AND OTHER ANIMALS/GERALD DURRELL

'What we all need,' said Larry, 'is sunshine...a country where we can *grow*.'

'Yes, dear, that would be nice,' agreed Mother, not really listening.

'I had a letter from George this morning – he says Corfu's wonderful. Why don't we pack up and go to Greece?'

'Very well, dear, if you like,' said Mother unguardedly.

Escaping the ills of the British climate, the Durrell family – acne-ridden Margo, gun-toting Leslie, bookworm Lawrence and budding naturalist Gerry, along with their long suffering mother and Roger the dog – take off for the island of Corfu. But the Durrells find that, reluctantly, they must share their various villas with a menagerie of local fauna – among them scorpions, geckos, toads, bats and butterflies.

Recounted with immense humour and charm *My Family and Other Animals* is a wonderful account of a rare, magical childhood.

'A bewitching book' *Sunday Times*

THE GREAT GATSBY/F. SCOTT FITZGERALD

'There was music from my neighbour's house through the summer nights. In his blue gardens men and girls came and went like moths among the whisperings and the champagne and the stars.'

Everybody who is anybody is seen at the glittering parties held in millionaire Jay Gatsby's mansion in West Egg, east of New York. The riotous throng congregates in his sumptuous garden, coolly debating Gatsby's origins and mysterious past. None of the frivolous socialites understands him and among various rumours is the conviction that 'he killed a man'. A detached onlooker, Gatsby is oblivious to the speculation he creates, but always seems to be watching and waiting, though no one knows what for.

As the tragic story unfolds, Gatsby's destructive dreams and passions are revealed, leading to disturbing consequences. A brilliant evocation of 1920s high society, *The Great Gatsby* peels away the layers of this glamorous world to display the coldness and cruelty at its heart.

'Not only a page-turner and a heartbreaker, it's one of the most quintessentially American novels ever written' *Time*

PENGUIN ESSENTIALS

CAT'S CRADLE/KURT VONNEGUT

'All of the true things I am about to tell you are shameless lies.'

Dr Felix Hoenikker, one of the founding fathers of the atomic bomb, has left a deadly legacy to the world. For he is the inventor of Ice-nine, a lethal chemical capable of freezing the entire planet. The search for its whereabouts leads to Hoenikker's three eccentric children, to a crazed dictator in the Caribbean, to madness.

Will Felix Hoenikker's death wish come true? Will his last, fatal gift to humankind bring about the end that, for all of us, is nigh?

Told with deadpan humour and bitter irony, Kurt Vonnegut's cult tale of global apocalypse preys on our deepest fears of witnessing the end and, worse still, surviving it . . .

'One of the warmest, wisest, funniest voices to be found anywhere in fiction'
Daily Telegraph

BRIDESHEAD REVISITED/EVELYN WAUGH

'I knew Sebastian by sight long before I met him. That was unavoidable for, from his first week, he was the most conspicuous man of his year by reason of his beauty, which was arresting, and his eccentricities of behaviour, which seemed to know no bounds.'

Charles Ryder, a lonely student at Oxford, is captivated by the outrageous and exquisitely beautiful Sebastian Flyte. Invited to Brideshead, Sebastian's magnificent family home, Charles welcomes the attentions of its eccentric, aristocratic inhabitants. But he also discovers a world where duty and desire, faith and earthly happiness are in conflict; a world which threatens to destroy his beloved Sebastian.

A scintillating depiction of the decadent, privileged aristocracy prior to the Second World War, *Brideshead Revisited* is widely regarded as Evelyn Waugh's finest work.

'A wildly entertaining, swooningly funny-sad story' *Time*

PENGUIN ESSENTIALS

The Penguin Essentials are some of the twentieth-century's most important books. When they were first published they changed the way we thought about literature and about life. And they have remained vital reading ever since. These new, stylish editions remind readers that once upon a time each book in the Essentials series was the only book worth being seen with.

Eva Luna by Isabel Allende

Out of Africa by Karen Blixen

A Clockwork Orange by Anthony Burgess

Breakfast at Tiffany's by Truman Capote

My Family and Other Animals by Gerald Durrell

The Great Gatsby by F. Scott Fitzgerald

A Room with a View by E.M. Forster

Cold Comfort Farm by Stella Gibbons

Goodbye to All That by Robert Graves

Steppenwolf by Hermann Hesse

On the Road by Jack Kerouac

Lady Chatterley's Lover by D.H. Lawrence

Lolita by Vladimir Nabokov

Wide Sargasso Sea by Jean Rhys

Bonjour Tristesse by Françoise Sagan

Hell's Angels by Hunter S. Thompson

A Confederacy of Dunces by John Kennedy Toole

Cat's Cradle by Kurt Vonnegut

Brideshead Revisited by Evelyn Waugh